Mahesh Dattani is a playwright, screenwriter, film-maker and stage director with several scripts and productions to his credit.

As a writer, he was awarded the prestigious Sahitya Akademi award in 1998. He has directed and scripted critically acclaimed films like *Mango Soufflé* and *Morning Raga*. His screenplays, along with his stage plays, have been published by Penguin.

Dattani is also a workshop facilitator for several writing and acting courses, having conducted workshops in many parts of the world, most notably at Portland State University in Oregon, USA. He has collaborated with international theatre companies like Border Crossings, most recently at Shanghai with Chinese, Swedish and English actors. He also writes scripts for BBC Radio 4.

His current works include a stage adaptation of Paulo Coelho's classic best-seller *The Alchemist* and also the script of *Brief Candle*, directed by Lillete Dubey.

PRAISE FOR MAHESH DATTANI

'Powerful and disturbing'—D.J.R. Bruckner, *The New York Times*

'A playwright of world stature'—Mario Relich, *Wasafiri*

'One of India's most serious and well-known playwrights writing on contemporary Indian themes'—Alexandra Viets, *The International Herald Tribune*

'At last we have a playwright who gives sixty million English-speaking Indians an identity'—Alyque Padamsee

BRIEF CANDLE

Three Plays

Mahesh Dattani

PENGUIN BOOKS

PENGUIN BOOKS
Published by the Penguin Group
Penguin Books India Pvt. Ltd, 7th Floor, Infinity Tower C, DLF Cyber City,
Gurgaon 122 002, Haryana, India
Penguin Group (USA) Inc., 375 Hudson Street, New York, New York 10014, USA
Penguin Group (Canada), 90 Eglinton Avenue East, Suite 700, Toronto, Ontario,
M4P 2Y3, Canada
Penguin Books Ltd, 80 Strand, London WC2R 0RL, England
Penguin Ireland, 25 St Stephen's Green, Dublin 2, Ireland (a division of Penguin
Books Ltd)
Penguin Group (Australia), 707 Collins Street, Melbourne, Victoria 3008, Australia
Penguin Group (NZ), 67 Apollo Drive, Rosedale, Auckland 0632, New Zealand
Penguin Books (South Africa) (Pty) Ltd, Block D, Rosebank Office Park, 181 Jan
Smuts Avenue, Parktown North, Johannesburg 2193, South Africa

Penguin Books Ltd, Registered Offices: 80 Strand, London WC2R 0RL, England

First published by Penguin Books India 2010

Copyright © Mahesh Dattani 2010
Copyright for the notes on the plays vests with the respective contributors

Thirty Days in September was first published by Penguin Books India in Collected
Plays Volume Two: Screen, Stage and Radio Plays 2005

ISBN 9780143415671

Typeset in Sabon Roman by SÜRYA, New Delhi
Printed at Repro India Ltd., Navi Mumbai

A PENGUIN RANDOM HOUSE COMPANY

For my mother Jaya Gowri.

The true token of her unconditional love was her patience and presence on opening ni hts!

CONTENTS

BRIEF CANDLE

A Dance between Love and Death

A Stage Play

A Note on the Play

Why do I write such heavy plays? This is a question that comes to me quite often, especially in the context of my two recent plays *Thirty Days in September* and *Brief Candle*. The question implies that the theatre is meant for lighter fare and nobody wants to go to the theatre to experience anything 'heavy' because life is heavy already. So in response to that question I can only ask another— 'Why do we lead such heavy lives?'

Without indulging in philosophical speculations, if we feel the unbearable heaviness of being, perhaps we can think of lessening the burden of stress, emotional turmoil, guilt or whatever it is that is adding to all that baggage that we carry around. So wouldn't it be a good idea if we at least acknowledged that burden in our plays or cinema? Why can't we allow theatre to do what it has been doing for thousands of years? Provide a pathway to our feelings and concerns so that we can look at life and its vicissitudes squarely in the mirror without having to wear a mask of placid existence?

In *Brief Candle* I have in fact attempted to work on that thin line that defines comedy from tragedy. In the play you have survivors of cancer who are in the process of putting up a comedy play as a fund-raiser for their hospice. Usually it is the mask of comedy that we tend to hide behind. In the play the mask of death is predominant almost to the point of ridicule. In that sense I do see the play more as a comedy with a flaw. As one of my characters puts it, 'In comedy, people don't die.' However, if we can view death with the same distance as we do comedy, then maybe it is not a comedy with a flaw anymore.

Thirty Days in September was written almost a decade ago, as a result of a commission from RAHI, a support group for people who have experienced sexual abuse in their childhood, mostly incest. At the time of writing it, there was no way I could look at a humorous side. To me, childhood sexual abuse seems too heinous a crime for me to even consider a funny side to it. There is no funny side. It is both a crime against the body as it is a crime against the mind. It is a play that continues to draw that question about writing heavy plays. It has sealed my fate as a 'serious' writer. I only have this to say in defence that writing comedy is serious business as well. In that sense every writer is a 'serious' one.

I am deeply indebted to Lillete Dubey and her Prime Time Theatre Company that produced these two plays. I am touched by Lillete's trust in me. She agreed to do *Thirty Days in September* even before she had read the complete play. As for *Brief Candle*, she announced the play even before I had written it. In return I trust her implicitly with her directorial vision and rarely have I intervened during her creative process with the actors. All creativity is about exploration, openness and a willingness to look at life again from a different perspective. It is rarely a result of flashes of genius but more an outcome of hard work, focus and unwavering passion. In that sense, my relationship with Lillete Dubey is always about exploring and creating spaces for the magic of theatre to happen.

Mahesh Dattani

Brief Candle was first performed on 5 July 2009 at ophia Bhabha Hall, Mumbai, by Prime Time Theatre Company witl the following cast in order of appearance:

DEEPIKA DAVE	Manasi Parekh
MAHESH TAWADE	Sachit Puranik
AMARINDER	Amar Talwar
AMOL	Joy Sengupta
SHANTI	Suchitra Pillai
VIKAS	Zafar Karchiwalo

Producer and Director	Lillete Dubey
Sets	Lillete Dubey anc Bhola Sharma
Lights	Inaayat Ali Sami
Costumes	Trishna Popat
Stage Manager	Altaf Sheikh

A composite set. A gauze curtain will separate spaces. The hotel rooms will remain the same except the number will change from 206 to 208.

One curtain partially covers a large 'Face of Cancer'. This is a large three-dimensional mask. A step can take the actor to a position above the head. The lower lip protrudes to become a bench on which an actor can sit.

Note: The Face of Cancer could be abstract, maybe an androgynous face that is melting. Hollow eyes, sallow skin, tufts of hair, etc. A face that is ravaged by the effects of chemotherapy and is now ready to give up the struggle.

On a high level or at the top of the Face, Vikas has a keyboard that he plays in different modes. Piano for the waltz, etc. At times he sets up a percussion groove for a scene.

SCENE I

Deepika Dave escorts Mahesh Tawade into Room 206.

DEEPIKA. Mr Kulkarni, this is your room which you will be sharing with a Mr Sengupta.

MAHESH. What are you saying? Me share a room?

DEEPIKA. It's only for the night—

MAHESH. Do you know who I am? Do you know—

DEEPIKA. Your flight will leave tomorrow morning at 6 a.m. so it's only a matter of—

MAHESH. Arre, what will you know? In Kolhapur they clear the runway for my private plane.

DEEPIKA. Well, this is Mumbai and it will take a few years before we get to where Kolhapur is—

MAHESH. And you want me to share my room with a—with a Sengupta?

DEEPIKA. I am sorry, but your airline was told in advance that we are overbooked—

MAHESH *(going to the phone)*. Call the airline right now—how can they treat us like this? *(Picking up the phone.)* Hello?

DEEPIKA. It's no use. The operator has not shown up. In fact none of the staff have shown up because of the storm.

> *Thunder and pouring rain. Deepika leaps and lands in Mahesh's arms.*

MAHESH *(letting go of her reluctantly)*. Oh! Oh, that is very—unfortunate. So we—you are all alone on this rainy night.

> *Deepika smiles coyly.*

DEEPIKA. Mr Sengupta is downstairs having a Bloody Mary.

MAHESH. Who is Mary?

DEEPIKA. A Bloody Mary—it's a—

MAHESH. And why are you abusing this Mary?

DEEPIKA. No, no. You have it all wrong. It's a drink.

MAHESH. I understand. When I get drunk I swear a lot too.

DEEPIKA. Look. You won't mind sharing this room, just for my sake, please?

MAHESH. For you I will do anything.

> *Mahesh advances towards her.*

DEEPIKA. Mr Kulkarni, wait—

MAHESH. Yes, yes! Mumbai girls like to talk first. We can talk about my private plane first. And then—

DEEPIKA. Oh no! I am not that type of person.

> *Mahesh tries to get his arms around her.*

DEEPIKA *(screaming)*. No!

Immediately the door pops open. Amarinder, a rugged looking man in his late fifties enters as if on cue.

AMARINDER. Did I hear a scream?

DEEPIKA. Yes, you did.

MAHESH. Mr Sengupta. This is my room and I want it all for myself. You can sleep with Mary in the bar.

AMARINDER. Oh, okay.

MAHESH. Okay? You have no problem?

AMARINDER. Why should I? I am not Mr Sengupta ... I was passing by and I heard a lady scream.

DEEPIKA. It's okay. It's okay.

AMARINDER. Actually I wanted to ask you something—since you are the manager.

MAHESH. Hands off! I saw her first.

AMARINDER. Er—the lady in 208. She bumped into me— accidentally. Well, I bumped into her.

Light on Shanti behind a screen. Music comes on and we see her moving about as if she is taking a shower.

AMARINDER. Well—I was wondering whether I could apologize to her. Will you ask her for me?

DEEPIKA. Okay.

AMARINDER. Good. And once I am in her room, could you have some wine sent in to the room, but don't take too long. But not if the 'Do Not Disturb' sign is turned on.

DEEPIKA. Mr Malhotra, you want me to set you up with Miss Unnikrishnan for the night?

MAHESH. What kind of a place is this? Sengupta having Mary in the bar and Malhotra having Miss Unnikrishnan in her room and me having the manager—

AMOL *(entering with a Bloody Mary in his hand and a strolley)*. Ho! This must be my room.

MAHESH. And Mr Sengupta in my room.

AMOL. Ah, madam, why did you leave me and go away?

AMARINDER. I hope you will oblige. I must rush now to—prepare myself. *(To Amol.)* You must be Mr Sengupta. We are on the same flight, we can leave together for the airport tomorrow.

AMOL. Ah, but we don't know when we are flying. Tomorrow, day after, or never.

MAHESH. I like that! I like that! So make the most of your stay at Hotel . . . *(To Deepika.)* Er—what's the name of the hotel?

DEEPIKA. Hotel Staylonger.

AMOL. Make the most of your stay in Hotel Staylonger, may your stay be long.

MAHESH. You mean short.

AMOL. No.

MAHESH. I am not going to spend more than one night with you!

AMOL. But what if my flight doesn't leave tomorrow?

DEEPIKA. You will be in trouble. Because the airline is paying for only one night, and you have exceeded your credit-card limit.

AMOL *(troubled)*. Where do I go? What do I do?

DEEPIKA. And we are out of Bloody Mary. So take good care of your drink.

Amol sips his drink very slowly.

DEEPIKA. All right. Drink it quickly so I can get you just one more. That's all we have.

Amol is reassured but still continues to drink it very slowly. Amarinder corners Mahesh.

AMARINDER *(whispering to Mahesh)*. Er—maybe you can help me out. You wouldn't have one of those pills would you?

MAHESH. Viagra?

AMARINDER. Shh!—I put mine in my checked-in baggage. I can't go out in this weather to buy it.

MAHESH *(smirking)*. And you can't get it up without it.

AMARINDER *(troubled)*. I can. I can! It's just that a—supplement will do me good. You see, I want to propose to Miss Unnikrishnan tonight before they announce her flight to Chennai, but first I want her to know how good I am in . . . How good I am at . . . You know—a real man.

MAHESH. A real man? A tiger?

Amarinder nods in enthusiasm.

DEEPIKA. Come on, drink up, Mr Sengupta. I haven't got all night.

MAHESH *(looking at Deepika)*. Yes, I do have one Viagra pill with me.

AMARINDER. You do? Oh, thank you! Thank you!

MAHESH *(winking and pointing at Deepika)*. But I am saving it for myself.

DEEPIKA. I heard that! I heard every word of what's going on and the answer is no!

AMOL. You will get me another Bloody Mary?

DEEPIKA. No!

AMOL. But you—

MAHESH. But you led me on!

DEEPIKA. I did not. You led yourself to believe . . . *(To Amarinder.)* And if you think you are going to score with Miss Unnikrishnan you have another thing coming.

AMARINDER. You don't know her at all!

DEEPIKA. Neither do you!

AMARINDER. I do! I bumped into her and you didn't!

DEEPIKA. Good luck! Don't say I didn't warn you.

AMOL. You promised me another—

DEEPIKA. No!

MAHESH. You promised me we will talk first about my private—

DEEPIKA. No!

Deepika's cellphone is ringing by now.

DEEPIKA *(into phone)*. I said NO!

The Face is revealed. Vikas is seated on top. He strikes a chord on the keyboard.

VIKAS. You promised me you will come to say goodbye.

Deepika is speechless. Everyone freezes on stage in their exaggerated gestures, while Deepika is in a spotlight.

Continues.

DEEPIKA. Go away!

VIKAS. You refuse to let me go.

DEEPIKA. I am telling you now to go!

VIKAS. Why didn't you come to see me when I was going?

DEEPIKA. I did come back but you were gone!

VIKAS. When you knew I was gone. You asked Mahesh whether I was gone before you came into the room.

DEEPIKA. Did he tell you that?

VIKAS. No. How could he? Not while I was dying.

DEEPIKA. He told you after you were gone.

VIKAS. Are you crazy? He doesn't talk to dead people.

The other actors unfreeze. Deepika is extremely troubled.

AMAR. Where is it? Give me my Viagra!

Begins to rummage the drawers.

MAHESH. It's not yours.

AMOL *(begging of Deepika)*. Oh please! Just one more Bloody Mary! Please! I will die if I don't get another one!

Mahesh is chasing Amarinder who is desperat ly looking for the pill. Amol squats on the floor nursin, an empty glass and begins to cry.

Shanti is dancing to herself in the shower and slowly the dance turns to a search for something on he1 body.

Deepika looks down on the action which gets more frantic. Amol's wailing, Amarinder's search Mahesh's attempts at stopping him get more physical a1d Shanti's body search gets more frantic.

DEEPIKA. Stop! Stop! Stop the rehearsal!

But the characters don't hear her as Vikas p1 1ys on.

Deepika goes to Shanti and stops her. Shanti eaches out for a tape and turns it off. All action comes to : standstill. Vikas softens on the keyboard.

Mahesh draws the curtain open.

DEEPIKA. We've done enough for today! The reh arsal is over. Amol, go back to your room. Tawade, clean up the room for the meeting with the interns.

AMAR. Shanti is the director of this play. She wil tell us when we pack up.

DEEPIKA. Shanti?

SHANTI *(after a while)*. All right, pack up. We m et tomorrow at 7.

Shanti and Amar are leaving. Amol stays c 1. Mahesh begins to set things back in place.

AMOL. I can understand why you are upset. Yo1 lose control over the situation, your feelings and, above ill, you lose control over the way you want us to look at ou. Doctors, patients, aides … Suddenly we are all being w ighed by the same scale.

SHANTI. You can't fight it. How can you not see i1 yourself? He has made it so clear!

Vikas laughs.

Shanti, Amar and Amol exit.

Deepika turns to Vikas.

DEEPIKA. What do you want from me? What???

Vikas comes out from behind the screen.

VIKAS. Mortmain.

DEEPIKA. Mortmain?

VIKAS. It means—

DEEPIKA. I know what it means. I told you what it means.

VIKAS. Ah, you do remember . . .

Vikas strums a sixties' or seventies' song. Lucy in the Sky with Diamonds.

The lights change.

We are in the past, on the terrace of their college.

Deepika joins in on the chorus of the song. Deepika has a joint with her. They share the joint in this scene. Vikas is more stoned than Deepika.

DEEPIKA. I love you. You know that.

VIKAS. What? *(Laughing.)*

DEEPIKA. Kiss me.

They kiss.

Vikas breaks away first, offers her the joint.

DEEPIKA. It's making me sick.

VIKAS. It's the best crap money can . . .

DEEPIKA. Vikas. What's all this about dropping out?

VIKAS. Do you really see me as a doctor? I mean healing people is cool, but all this medical degree and stuff. For what? Start a clinic? You and I bound till eternity to some shitty building? I'd rather just go where I want to or where I am needed.

DEEPIKA. So you joined medical college because your father wanted you to? What happened to your rebellion then?

VIKAS. It seemed like a good idea at that time. I do want to help the world move. But I can do that now. Why waste three years in this shithole?

DEEPIKA. And—what about us?

VIKAS. Come with me.

DEEPIKA. Be a dropout? Like you? . . . You know I won't do it. You are dumping me.

VIKAS. Hey, hang on . . .

DEEPIKA. You just want out! From me!

Vikas looks at her for a while and then begins singing again.

DEEPIKA. I—I am going to be sick! Just go!

Deepika leaves.

Blackout.

SCENE II

Vikas continues to play. The scene is now the hospice. Mahesh is taking out his tablets from a box with compartments. Vikas is now a patient in the ward.

VIKAS. Come, sit here.

MAHESH. Now please don't make me sit and talk. You are not the only one here . . . (*Offering the pills with water on a tray.*) If you want one more Roxanol, I will give it to you.

VIKAS. Oh. So you do a side business of selling drugs? How much?

MAHESH. What are you saying, sir? These are doctor's orders.

Deepika enters. Tawade rises.

DEEPIKA. Where is Sister Parvati?

Without waiting for an answer she picks up a chart.

DEEPIKA. What's this?

VIKAS *(taking away his papers).* Oh that. Just a play I am writing.

DEEPIKA. Why is it clipped on to your medical report? . . . What kind of play?

VIKAS. About us. Our past. How we—

DEEPIKA. Tawade!! *(She gestures for him to leave.)*

Tawade leaves.

VIKAS. How we made passionate love on the terrace of our college. *(Laughing.)* Relax. I was just pulling your leg. It's just a comedy.

DEEPIKA. Mortmain.

VIKAS. Huh?

DEEPIKA. A hand from the past . . . A dead hand.

Pause.

DEEPIKA. If writing makes you feel better, go ahead. But remember, I am a doctor and you are in my hospice.

VIKAS. One day you will act in my play. There is a role in it for you. I will touch you with this play of mine. From the dead. *(Gesturing to touch her.)* Mortmain.

Deepika finds it difficult to continue with this conversation.

DEEPIKA. Take your medication on time. You won't feel the pain. *(Yelling.)* Tawade!

Deepika walks out as Tawade re-enters.

Tawade gives him the tablet.

Vikas puts it away in his pocket.

MAHESH. Give it to me. If you are not taking the tablet I have to put it back.

VIKAS. Don't tell her I didn't take it.

MAHESH. What goes of my father's? What are you saving it for? So you can take them all at once and die?

VIKAS *(leaning over)*. When I want to die, I think I will just jump off this—

MAHESH. If you try to do such things, I will tell her and your hands will be tied to the bed. That is what we do to people who pull out their feeding tubes or run to the balcony to jump . . .

VIKAS. If they want to die, why don't you let them?

MAHESH. You come down now.

VIKAS. No. I like it here. Are you worried I will jump? Not that anything goes of your father's if I die. Except, you will have to clean up the mess. That is what you are thinking of, right?

MAHESH. Please come into the room now. Enough of all this.

VIKAS. First tell me. Am I right? When you saw me trying to jump you were thinking, now I will have to clean the blood and god knows what else. Right?

Mahesh is uneasy.

VIKAS. Right or wrong?

MAHESH. Please. Not today. I have to go to Bajrang Bali temple. Please. I won't tell Doctor that you did not take Roxanol. Please. Tomorrow. Do it tomorrow, when Samant is on duty.

VIKAS. Bajrang Bali. What are you praying to Hanumanji for?

MAHESH. Just like that. He is my God!

VIKAS *(making to leap off the balcony)*. Jai Bajrang Bali!

MAHESH. No!

VIKAS. My friend is a truck driver. He told me why he prays to Bajrang Bali. While driving the truck he gets so horny that he can't drive straight. So he prays to Bajrang Bali to give him strength to control himself. At least till the next stop. That is your problem, right?

MAHESH. No! I am not a truck driver! I don't drive! I just move from room to room, or sit in the corner and try to sleep!

VIKAS. You are a bachelor, right?

MAHESH. Yes.

VIKAS. So am I. But you don't go around screwing like I did. You just sit in a corner. Like Little Jack Horny.

MAHESH. Yes! That's why I don't have AIDS!

Pause.

VIKAS. Come here.

Mahesh gets on to the step gingerly and sits next to Vikas. Vikas rests his head on his shoulder. Mahesh, after a moment, puts his arm around him, patting his arm.

VIKAS. That's what I needed. Just a touch. But she would rather give me extra morphine.

Pause.

VIKAS. I see you. Every time she leans over to examine me, you are staring at her. Sometimes you stand in front of her and sometimes—you prefer the view from the back.

Mahesh does not quite know what to say or do.

VIKAS. And that's why you pray to Lord Hanuman, eh? To give you strength?

MAHESH. You have gone mad!

VIKAS. She is an attractive woman. Wouldn't you like to marry her?

MAHESH. Where am I and where is she?

VIKAS. So you would like to be where she is?

MAHESH. A doctor? No, no.

VIKAS. A rich man, then. I will make you a rich man and I will make sure she falls for you.

Amol enters and stands at the base of the face. He is holding an almost empty bottle of blood which is going into his veins through a tube. His posture is similar to the one he held when he had a glass of Bloody Mary in his hand. He overhears the rest.

VIKAS. In return, just love me the same way while I die.

MAHESH. You should not want people to love you when you are going. You won't want to go then.

VIKAS. Then what, in your opinion, should people who are going want?

MAHESH. Pray for freedom from the cycle of life and death. Do you know the Hanuman Chalisa? If you recite that a hundred times every day you will be free forever.

VIKAS. But I want to live.

MAHESH. Hmm ... Then chant the Maha Mrityunjaya.

VIKAS. Ah! Like Markandeya. *Om Trayambakam Yajamahe* ... What was his story?

MAHESH. You know the story.

VIKAS. But tell me again. I want to hear it.

MAHESH. I'm not your grandmother.

VIKAS. Tell me, otherwise I will tell Dr Dave that you're always looking at ...

MAHESH. All right! Once there was a sage who did not have a son.

VIKAS. Did he have a daughter?

MAHESH. I don't know, sahib.

VIKAS. Anyway, they don't count in these stories. Go on.

MAHESH. Do you want to listen to the story?

VIKAS. Yes, yes, go on.

MAHESH. The sage prayed to Lord Shiva for a son, Lord Shiva was pleased and he granted him his wish. But he gave him a choice. Either a bad son who would live for a hundred years, or a good and devout son who would only live till he was sixteen. Naturally the sage chose the good and devout son and hence Markandeya, the perfect son, was born. But on his sixteenth birthday, Yamaraj, the God of death, came to get Markandeya.

VIKAS. Bad man, bad man!

MAHESH. The boy clung onto Lord Shiva's statue and prayed, '*Om Trayambakam Yajamahe . . .*' Shiva was pleased with his devotion, so he made sure the boy never turned sixteen, so Yama could not take him away . . . So you choose now. Do you want freedom from the cycle of life and death? Chant Hanuman Chalisa. If you want to cling on to life, then chant Maha Mrityunjaya.

Vikas sits up and looks at Mahesh.

VIKAS. You are so wise and wonderful. For that my friend, I will make you a rich man.

MAHESH *(excited)*. Really? How?

VIKAS. If you were rich, what would you want? Apart from a beautiful woman.

MAHESH. I want a private plane.

VIKAS. What??? A private plane?

MAHESH. Yes!

VIKAS. What will you do if you had one?

MAHESH. In my town, my grandfather's rival has become a politician. They have a private plane. They don't even look at us now. If I had a private plane I will take my grandfather and grandmother to all four Dhams in my plane, just to show those worthless sons of bitches that I am also somebody . . .

VIKAS. You shall have it!

MAHESH *(wide-eyed)*. Really? How? You will leave all your money to me in your will?

AMOL. He doesn't have even ten thousand rupees in his bank!

MAHESH *(coming down)*. Amol sahib! What are you doing? If you leave your bed again, I will tie your hands!

AMOL *(to Vikas)*. And you! Why are you raising that man's hopes? *(To Mahesh.)* Tawade, stop all this day dreaming. And get this tube out of my veins.

MAHESH *(pushing him gently)*. First you come bacl to your bed.

AMOL *(to Vikas)*. If you really want to be of use, lo something to help me. I can't get any more drugs. My ins irance won't pay anymore! I don't want to die on the street!

Amol hits out at Mahesh who was trying to et him in.
Amol begins to weep. Vikas comes down to hi 1 and gives
him the Roxanol tablet.

VIKAS. Hang on and somebody will help.

Vikas collapses.

Blackout. Mahesh chants the Maha Mrityunj ya.

Spotlight picks up Vikas in bed, breathing ha d.

Beside him are Shanti, Amar, Amol and Mah sh.

VIKAS. Doctor! . . . Where is she? Where the fuc is she?

SHANTI *(to Mahesh)*. Fetch her. Now!

Mahesh goes to Deepika, standing in a sepa ate space.
Deepika is troubled and we can see it is a tou h decision
for her to make.

MAHESH. Doctor, please.

DEEPIKA. Give him more morphine.

MAHESH. He doesn't want it, he wants—

DEEPIKA. There is nothing I can do! Let me kno / when he is gone.

Deepika exits.

VIKAS. Where are you?

We are in the rehearsal room. Present. His hea / breathing
comes to a stop.

Blackout. Mahesh continues with the Stotra t ll the next
scene begins.

SCENE III

Deepika speaks, trying to keep it professional.

DEEPIKA. I did have a word with the committee. We have collectively arrived at the decision that we should do something else. So, you see. It's not just me who feels that way.

SHANTI. They wanted a comedy, we will give them one. Vikas wrote this as a comedy and that is the way we will play it. No one except us will understand that it's about—

Shanti stops speaking as she looks at Deepika.

SHANTI. About something else. Deepika is upset.

Amol, who is reading the script, laughs.

AMOL. He is funny.

DEEPIKA. It might disturb you and I am concerned.

AMARINDER. Dr Dave. How dare you?

Silence.

DEEPIKA. What exactly do you mean by that?

AMARINDER. You have counselled each one of us and one of the things, if not the one thing, that you stressed upon was to let it all out. To talk, to learn to forgive, to see yourself and love yourself.

DEEPIKA. This is not about counselling. He was not a counsellor. He was a passionate man with strong views on everything and everybody. He knew he was dying. He felt strongly about each one of us. So he put it all down. *(Holding up the script.)* This is about him, not us. Now, it is no longer about him. It should be about us. I don't want any of you to live your life through his eyes.

AMARINDER. He was a good counsellor. That's how he got to know us so well.

DEEPIKA. Did he really know you?

AMARINDER. He understood what I was going through. Far

better than you did. Maybe because he was a man. No, not true. My urologist is a man and he doesn't understand what is going on in my mind. Vikas knew. He knew the moment he saw me.

Vikas appears strumming a guitar. At the top of the fret is tied a mask similar to the face. It dangles and dances almost to the music, sometimes in front of the actors.

AMARINDER. My first stay at the hospital. The biopsy was made and I woke up feeling sore inside. I don't know how I allowed it. They never told me that they will be drilling inside my body. At my core. What made me a man? Climbing a mountain, playing a game of hockey, knowing I could satisfy a woman in bed. All that was under attack with a group of needles probing at my prostate, through the wall of my rectum. Like being sodomized with metal. *(Staring at the mask dangling in Vikas's hand.)* I rang for the nurse but nobody came. I lay there thinking of the results of that biopsy. If I did have cancer, they will remove my prostate. A gland the size of a walnut that defines my maleness. What will I choose? To live? And deal with the loss? Instead of vitality flowing through my loins, bear the embarassment of urine dribbling down my pants and not even noticing it? I wanted to live! With everything I had!

Vikas hums the Maha Mrityunjay accompanied by his guitar.

AMARINDER. I got up and staggered out of my room. And I saw what I was fearing the most . . . I almost fell on to a passing stretcher. It appeared as if they were taking away a dead body. I recoiled. It was the memory of my wife. One minute she was singing and dancing and the next . . . they were taking her away on a stretcher. But this time the face was uncovered.

The mask dangles near Shanti's face.

AMARINDER. I tried to focus. On the stretcher was a face that was alive after having seen hell. *(Looking at the mask in front of Shanti's face.)* She was unconscious but her lips were pursed as if she wanted to say something—that she was in a similar place as I.

SHANTI. Vikas had promised to be there. I was conscious but could not speak. I reached out for Vikas. For anybody. My sister was on her way. She was stuck somewhere in Frankfurt while my body was agitated with all the radiation and I had no one to hold on to. Vikas knew that and he promised to be there. I reached out for him.

VIKAS. I was there, but you reached out for Amar.

SHANTI. I thought it was you. I was expecting you.

Vikas moves to Amarinder humming softly.

SHANTI. But I saw Amar. I saw Fear. The same fear that I had. It wasn't the fear of death. It was the fear of . . .

Amarinder holds the mask that is near him.

AMARINDER. It was the fear—that . . .

VIKAS. It is the fear of losing something that you have and did not even think of the possibility of not having. But now when there is a real danger of losing it, you begin to understand its true worth. And then you are afraid you will have to live without it for the rest of your living moments.

Vikas moves away, singing softly.

SHANTI. He knew.

AMARINDER. He knew what was going on in our heads.

AMOL. He once asked me what I thought of Amar and his decision to die.

MAHESH. He asked me also. I told him straight away that he has to live. But what a life to live!

Mahesh clucks in sympathy.

AMARINDER (*to Mahesh*). Enough! It is that kind of sympathy that I cannot bear to see in other men! I envy you. I envy you your life and your health. But please don't pity me!

MAHESH. But you must try to live! Both Vikas Sir and Amol Sir told me that they wanted to live. Amol Sir, how can you think that it is better for him to die? You yourself said you did not want to—

Amol takes the mask from its string and wears it quickly.

AMOL. I just wish to be left alone. I have no desire apart from doing this play. It is funny! He is making us laugh! At ourselves, at others. Just having a good laugh. And I know somewhere that I was part of his inspiration. *(Laughing.)* I just love the bit where he is drunk from all the Bloody Mary and doesn't know which room he is in! Right till the end, he doesn't have a place to stay in Hotel Staylonger. *(Laughing.)* And Kulkarni thinks he is having an affair with Mary!

Amol almost falls off his chair laughing.

Vikas takes off the mask from Amol.

AMOL *(going to Deepika)*. You are not dying. Yet you think only of yourself and not your patients.

DEEPIKA. That is unfair.

AMOL. You are forced to, right? I mean, being a doctor you can't really be too sensitive.

Vikas dangles the mask in front of Deepika like a pendulum.

AMOL. You have to treat everyone like a rotting tree that is about to fall. You are interested in the tree only till the rot is removed. The tree survives or the tree falls down once the rot is taken out. You wait to see what happens. And then, on to the next day.

DEEPIKA *(nodding)*. Maybe so. Maybe so ...

AMOL. Thanking God that you don't have the rot within you.

DEEPIKA. Yes.

AMOL. Ah, but you never know ...

DEEPIKA *(nodding, looking at the mask)*. You never know.

AMOL. But to him, we were more than just rotting trees.

Silence.

DEEPIKA. He chose to come here. He had very high expectations of me. I failed him, and so he wrote this play. He is angry with me. And I refuse to be a victim of his anger.

VIKAS. That is not the whole story. Tell them everything.

SHANTI. It is hardly an angry play.

VIKAS *(caressing her hair)*. You never touched me once when I was ill.

AMOL. I can only see laughter, not anger.

VIKAS. You can touch me now. Do the play. I long for your touch.

DEEPIKA. I don't want to be touched!

AMARINDER. It is a touching play too.

DEEPIKA *(pushing Vikas's hand away)*. I don't want to be touched!

AMOL *(laughing)*. In a tickly sort of way!

Deepika continues to resist Vikas's caresses.

SHANTI. It's funny all the way! Even his emails were so funny. Here is the last one he sent. *(Reading a note attached to her script.)* 'Dear Shanti. You did once say to me that you are a film-maker. I have written the script for your first feature film. Ta Dah! If I am dead by the time you move your butt and make it, send the millions in royalty to Mahesh Tawade to help him with his down payment for an aeroplane.'

They all laugh. Deepika gives in and allows Vikas to caress her.

DEEPIKA. I cannot give in to this. I am in charge here. This is my project and this is my hospice!

AMARINDER. I understand. It must be painful for you. And I thought you were the healthy one amongst us.

AMOL. Surely there is a lot more than you are telling us.

SHANTI. It's okay, Amol. Let her be.

DEEPIKA *(to Amol)*. That is none of your business!

Amol is silenced by that stern remark.

Deepika moves to Shanti.

DEEPIKA. He told you.

Shanti nods.

DEEPIKA. You think I am heartless. You think I led him on.

SHANTI. He never said that.

DEEPIKA. But you think so.

Shanti nods.

DEEPIKA. And that's the real reason why you wanted to do this. To teach me a lesson.

SHANTI. No. I admire your strength.

DEEPIKA. Then why?!

SHANTI. I promised him that I will help you—live through his absence.

Deepika is shocked by this remark. She feels vulnerable.

DEEPIKA. I am not in mourning! I am not suffering in silence! I can live through his absence like I can live through the absence of any of the ones who don't make it!

Silence.

MAHESH. He is not absent! He does not want to go! He is clinging on! To us!

SHANTI. To you!

Vikas begins to chant loudly.

Vikas's voice trails off as he looks at the others lost in a long silence.

Fade to black.

SCENE IV

*It is Miss Unnikrishnan's room. Shanti is brushing her
hair singing a Hindi film song.*

SHANTI *(humming)*. *Paani mein jale, paani mein jale mera gora
badan* . . .

There is a deliberate knock on the door.

SHANTI *(putting a hand to her bosom)*. Oh! That must be room
service. I hope he is handsome! *(Calling in a sing-song voice.)*
Come in!

Amarinder comes into the room.

AMARINDER. Oh, Miss Unnikrishnan! I am extremely sorry to
disturb you, but may I take a little bit of your—ahem—time.

SHANTI *(giggling like a girl)*. Okay. Just a little bit at a time.

AMARINDER. Well, I just wanted to apologize for—bumping into
you in the lobby . . . I hope you will forgive me for that.

SHANTI. Oh, is that all? I must apologize too, for my strong
reaction. You see I was brought up very strictly. But now, of
course, I am a lot more loose—loosened up.

AMARINDER. Me too! Er—may I have a glass of water. I need
to—

*Amarinder takes out a pill. He looks around, half expecting
someone to take it away.*

Mahesh bursts into the room.

MAHESH. No, don't take that!

*Amarinder grabs the glass of water while Mahesh tries to
stop him. Shanti screams. Amarinder manages to swallow
the pill.*

AMARINDER. Aha! Now you can't have it. Thank you. One day
I will repay you for this. Now go and leave us alone.

SHANTI. You are not room service! Go away!

MAHESH. Madam, you are in trouble.

AMARINDER. No! We just need to wait for half an hour and you will be in heaven!

MAHESH. Within half an hour you will be dead That was a cyanide capsule.

AMARINDER. What?

Shanti screams.

MAHESH. Quickly! Get it out before it dissolves!

AMARINDER (*rushing to the bathroom*). It looked ke Viagra to me!

Shanti faints in Mahesh's arms.

MAHESH. No! It's okay. Wake up. I was only jo ing.

Mahesh is carrying the fainted Shanti on to t e bed. We hear retching sounds from the bathroom.

MAHESH. That man will die anyway if he takes so nuch Viagra.

Amol bursts into the room.

AMOL. Where is the key to my room? You have l cked me out of my room. Give me my key!

MAHESH. It's my room! Go speak to the manage for another room.

AMOL. No, I will not! I will stand up for my rig ts! I will not have you evict me from my room while you re molesting Miss Unnikrishnan.

More retching sounds from the bathroom.

MAHESH. I am not molesting her! She fainted wh en she heard it wasn't Viagra he had!

AMOL. Give me the key!

Amol begins to search in Mahesh's kurta pock t. Mahesh resists. Shanti sits up and screams again as st e sees two men fighting.

Amarinder comes in with gusto.

AMARINDER. There! I have gotten rid of it. Now get lost.

MAHESH. Aha! Fooled you. It was Viagra. Serves you right for stealing it from me. Come on, Mr Sengupta, let us go to my room.

AMOL. My room!

MAHESH. Come on! Let's find Mary first.

AMOL *(while leaving).* Yes, find me a Bloody Mary.

MAHESH *(offstage).* Again you are cursing that poor girl.

AMARINDER *(shutting the door).* Aha! Fooled him! I knew it was Viagra! I heard him say that. *(Winking at Shanti.)* I pretended to throw up. *(Patting his stomach.)* It's in me. And it is working!

Amarinder hugs her suddenly. She gasps.

AMARINDER. What is the matter? Am I too rough for you?

SHANTI. Oh no! I broke my strap!

Shanti breaks away and covers her left breast with a hand towel.

AMARINDER. Never mind.

SHANTI. Oh no! All my clothes are checked in! What will I wear on the flight?

Deepika knocks on the door.

DEEPIKA. Room service! Your champagne.

Deepika puts the pail down by the bed.

SHANTI. I didn't order champagne.

AMARINDER. It must be on the house.

DEEPIKA. It isn't! Nothing is on the house.

AMARINDER. We will settle that later.

SHANTI. Maybe you can help.

DEEPIKA. Why does everyone want my help?

AMARINDER. Yes, go away!

SHANTI. No. Can you give me one of yours? I mean mine is broken.

DEEPIKA. You should be more careful with your things.

SHANTI. No, no. It's my strap. It just came off.

Shanti sneezes. Unintentionally the towel slips off Shanti's breast. Amarinder is right in front of her. He recoils involuntarily.

AMARINDER. Oh my God!

Silence, as Shanti backs away.

AMARINDER. I—I am sorry. I did't mean to—

Shanti is almost in tears. She leaves.

AMARINDER. Shanti . . .

DEEPIKA. It's okay.

AMARINDER. No, it's not!

Amarinder leaves.

Fade out.

SCENE V

The lights pick up Shanti at the Face, sitting in the mouth cradle.

SHANTI. On my wedding night, my husband put on some music and danced. He wanted me to dance with him. I wasn't prepared for that. My mother had told me that I should on no account show any enthusiasm but follow his instructions. But I should also know when to gently protest, and when to finally give in . . . She never told me he would want to dance with me on my wedding night. Maybe it didn't cross her mind, otherwise she would have put me through dancing lessons at the age of seven. She put me through Carnatic music. I sang well and I had sung for him when he had come to see me. He was impressed with my singing, and also our ancestral home in Mylapore . . . He brought me to Matunga. I could see why he liked our home. His flat was maybe just a bit bigger than our servant's rooms. Now my flat . . . The tape played a waltz. I watched him dance and I remembered the song from *Pyaasa* where Guru Dutt and Mala Sinha waltzed in a dream sequence ... On my wedding night, dressed in heavy silk and jewellery, he wanted me to dance. I tried to get my mother's voice out of my ears—I certainly did not want to give in. Finally I said no. I did not want to make a fool of myself, not on my wedding night. He gave up after a while. He looked a bit silly too, waltzing all by himself. He began to caress me as I lay frozen. I didn't feel anything. He began to unbutton my blouse. I moved away. I wasn't being coy ... How could I? I hadn't seen my own breast in the mirror. In the bathroom, I always took off my blouse when I was away from the mirror. How could I to this—man? He was patient. He waited for two days. Then I let him embrace me, but I could not show myself to him. Ever ...

Silence.

SHANTI. Our maid showed me the blood stains on my brassiere. She thought I had hurt myself. She told my mother-in-law. She insisted I go for a test ... I lay exposed to the technicians, my breast pushed against the X-ray plate. One of them marked my lumps, treating my breast as if it were already a piece of dead flesh ... At least I could say no to Mukund, but the doctors, lab technicians ... Their job was to invade my body and take out tumours, and they did. But they grew and came back till they took it all out. A part of me that I had barely felt. That I had never seen fully myself. Gone.

Amarinder enters.

AMARINDER. I just want you to know that I understand.

SHANTI. How could you?

AMARINDER. It can't be that different.

SHANTI. It cannot be that similar. You don't know. You can't possibly know!

AMARINDER. Maybe so ...

SHANTI. Please leave me alone.

AMARINDER. Of course.

As Amarinder is leaving.

SHANTI. Same attitude as before.

AMARINDER. Huh?

SHANTI. Maybe I deliberately let that towel fall. To see your reaction.

AMARINDER. No, you didn't.

SHANTI. I didn't. But I am glad it happened. At least I know.

AMARINDER. No. You don't know.

SHANTI. That look on your face. When I first looked up at you on that stretcher after my third chemo session, I reached out because I thought I was dead. And you were some divine being who would help me across. I was alive, and there was nothing divine about the fear on your face. After that we talked. You told me what you were going through. You say you can understand me. I hope then you understand that I regret all the years I spent not knowing how to love myself. My body, my self. Now I want to love myself but I don't. I thought we could talk about that now. And about us. But . . . I see the same man I did when I reached out. A man eaten by fear.

AMARINDER. You reached out to me, but I let you down. I could only see my own fate. I can understand you and you will understand me if we give each other some time. I thought I was strong, now. Yes. I am afraid, even more so than before. Not of dying. I have to deal with it. I admire you. At least you are taking a good look in the mirror now.

That is why I want to do this play. To take a good look at myself . . . Whether I choose not to have the surgery and die. Or live without really living. I thought you would help me make my decision. But you have your own needs. That's why I feel I can understand. It is not me who you see as insensitive. It is still about your husband.

Vikas plays music. A waltz.

Fade to:

SCENE VI

*We are now back at rehearsals. Amarinder is dancing.
Shanti walks towards him. She picks up the towel and
places it on her shoulder. She does not dance with him.
She is now watching as a director would, but clearly she
is reflecting on the incident in her own life.*

AMARINDER. It's working! Less than half an hour. I must be
getting better! I am getting better! Better! Best!

*Amarinder clutches at his heart and collapses after a long
drawn-out groan.*

SHANTI. I scream. *(Louder.)* Scream!

Amol and Mahesh come in.

AMOL. What happened?

MAHESH. We are here to protect you. Where is the bastard? I
will kill him.

SHANTI *(getting into the act).* Oh no! He vanished before he
could rob me of my youth!

Mahesh props him up on the bed.

AMOL. Oh no! You killed the man.

SHANTI. I did not. He did it all by himself.

AMOL. And you just stood there and let it happen. You just
watched him die!

MAHESH. He is dying.

AMOL. He is dead, you mean.

MAHESH. No. No. He is dying.

SHANTI. He is alive, you mean.

MAHESH. Yes. If he is dying he must be alive.

SHANTI. But not for long.

AMOL. Unless we stop him from dying.

SHANTI. There's a thought.

MAHESH. How?

SHANTI. Somebody call a doctor!

Shanti runs to the door and yells.

SHANTI. Is there a doctor in this hotel? Doctor! Doctor!

Deepika appears.

SHANTI (*dragging her in*). Oh thank God, you are here.

DEEPIKA. But what is the matter.

SHANTI. He is dying.

DEEPIKA. What? In my hotel?

SHANTI. Help save him, if you don't want him to die in your hotel.

DEEPIKA. How?

AMOL. Find a doctor or be one.

DEEPIKA. But what is wrong with him?

MAHESH. Too much Viagra and too little sex.

DEEPIKA. What can I do?

MAHESH. Kiss him.

DEEPIKA. What?

AMOL. Yes, a kiss always works.

DEEPIKA. Why can't Miss Unnikrishnan kiss him? She brought it on.

SHANTI. I did not! We were dancing and he just—

DEEPIKA. Go ahead, Miss Unnikrishnan. What have you got to lose?

AMOL. Yes, and do it fast. He is sinking.

MAHESH. Go on.

SHANTI. With all of you watching?

MAHESH. We will shut our eyes. Now do it. Quickly! Everyone close your eyes!

Everyone shuts their eyes and makes a point of looking away.

Shanti kisses Amarinder.

The waltz begins to play again.

Amarinder gets up.

AMARINDER. Darling! I can see again.

SHANTI. Oh my darling! I am so happy I could cry!

AMARINDER. Come on, let's complete the dance we started.

Amarinder begins to dance.

SHANTI. I can't! I can't!

Shanti weeps.

The waltz continues. The lights change.

The others continue to walk with their eyes shut, groping as if in the dark.

Shanti continues to cry now for real.

During the waltz, Vikas, with his death mask on, dances with Amarinder for a while. Amar looks at the death mask and recoils as before, but slowly begins to dance.

Vikas leaves him and holds a weeping Shanti, comforting her.

Deepika and Mahesh are groping, like in the dark. Their hands meet. They recoil. Amol finds himself near the mask and begins to feel it part by part. Mahesh leads Vikas to Deepika. Deepika begins to feel his shoulder. But when she comes to the mask she recoils. This entire action is in a loop, starting from when Amarinder begins to dance. It rewinds and repeats itself without Amol. Amol is near the mask as he talks to the audience. The waltz replay is much softer now. Amol speaks while the actions continue. He occasionally looks at them.

AMOL. 98-99-100. Ready or not, I am coming! ... *(Looking around.)* I spy Flora! I spy Flora! *(To audience.)* My cousins were Flora and Fauna. Do you find the names a little odd? You do? You are definitely not a Bengali. Saraswati Pishi thought they were cute. Pagol Pishi, we called her. I hated my pet name. Bunki. But when we all met up at our ancestral home in Bolpur a name like Bunki did not stand out from Flora, Fauna, Topkapi, Bullu, Pochka ... I would have been ostracized if my parents had named me Rahul. So we played away our summers—I spy, blind man's buff, holly colly, football. Each one of us laughing and fighting when together but holding back some little secret ... Some fear, laughing louder so our secret will go unnoticed. Hiding ourselves so that no one can say, 'I spy Bunki! He has a pimple on his bum!' Or, 'I spy Bunki! He is afraid of the dark!' Or, 'I spy Bunki! His father beats him up when he is angry.' *(Walking among the others.)* I was twelve when we moved from Kolkata. My father did not get along well with his family. So he took his share and left for Delhi. I never saw my ancestral home again. *(Playing 'I spy'.)* Where is Bunki? Bunki is hiding somewhere! Okay, we give up, Bunki. Come on out. Bunki! Where are you?

Amol looks around like the rest as if groping in the dark.

AMOL. Bunki had gone forever. Where are you? Ah, I spy. There he is, doing a street play. Jan Natya Manch. Very Marxist, very passionate. Now he is on the street but he is not doing a street play. Yet he is on the street. With his mother. One day his mother had gone shopping. And when she came back, the watchman did not allow her into her own building. She shouted and screamed. A man came out and told her to get out. Our father had married that man's sister and now it was her house. *(Looking helplessly at the others as they go about their actions.)* Help. Somebody help us, please. Both of us without a home. *(Darts around the group as if looking for the people he is talking about.)* Nowhere to hide. Her sister. Neelima Mashi. Day job, night college. Finally I spy Rose. Rosalynd. We danced, we made love, we married. The happiest time of my life. Until, until, one day ...

Amol begins to cough.

The music stops. The actors pause. They look at Amol coughing.

VIKAS *(with his mask on).* Aha! I spy Bunki! I spy!

Silence. Vikas walks slowly towards Amol. Amol looks at the mask, scared.

AMOL. Don't tell Rose.

VIKAS. She knows. She has seen the reports.

Silence.

AMOL. Why me?

VIKAS. You are not very good at hiding. Even little Flora could catch you. And I am a big boy.

The others walk slowly towards the periphery.

AMOL. You see. My insurance is not going to last long. And I don't want Rose to work any harder than she is. So hide me. Please.

Vikas nods. Amol dashes and hides behind him. After a while Amol peeps from behind Vikas.

AMOL. Is she gone?

VIKAS. Congratulations. She didn't catch you.

Amol comes out. Deepika steps forward.

DEEPIKA. Amol, I am sorry but there is nothing I can do. We cannot treat you any longer. The hospice is full.

AMOL. Okay. I will then - just look for another place to . . .

Deepika circles around Vikas and Amol.

AMOL. Vikas. Why are you smiling?

Deepika is back again at the same spot.

DEEPIKA. Amol, I am happy to tell you that we can offer you treatment. Somebody has paid for your stay too. You have a benefactor.

Amol looks at Vikas.

AMOL *(to Vikas)*. You old bastard. You did have the money! Thank you. Oh thank you! You saved my—

Amol catches himself from saying 'You saved my life'.

Vikas softly hums the Maha Mrityunjaya mantra.

AMOL. It's my turn next. I know. Maybe, after the play. I'll see you again, after the show.

Amol exits.

Vikas looks at Deepika.

DEEPIKA. Do you think I could, somehow, get rid of you?

VIKAS. If only you had said goodbye. Don't you regret that?

DEEPIKA. Oh come on! Regret? You just show up one day— sick. Deepika, nursemaid, take care of me now. Hug me now, and love me. Why? Because you were dying? Because you are a man and I am a woman? It's my job to nurture you? Because you have no one else? Where were all the whores, truck drivers, beggars you spent so much time with? Why didn't you ask them to hold you and touch you now? Why me? Everyone sympathizes with you because you are dead. You are the one who lived a colourful life. A free-thinking, free-moving writer who warmed the cockles of people's hearts! Everyone says, 'Oh, he changed my life. He showed me how to live. Why do good people like Vikas have to go?' I am the bad person. Oh, dead people are all saints! Living people are bad, bad, bad. Where were you when I needed you?

VIKAS. I was travelling, making friends.

DEEPIKA. Oh sure! More orgies.

VIKAS. You can't make me feel bad about anything. And you can't get away with the fact that you just disappeared. Without a word. I thought okay, at least I had something special in college with you. I could get by on that.

Deepika is about to respond but he interrupts her.

VIKAS. After just a month of our separation, in Kalimpong I bump into our old classmate Timok.

Deepika stiffens.

VIKAS. We got talking and he mentioned that you were seeing someone. You were sleeping with him even when we were together! I wasn't so special after all. Why? Why did you do that?

DEEPIKA. What did you want? That I should stay faithful while you believed in free love? I knew it wouldn't work between us. I was preparing myself for a fall. With you, I didn't feel loved. I looked at you and saw that you were attracted to me. But when you talked about travelling and meeting farmers and field workers your eyes would light up in a special way. That is where you were going. I knew even before you dropped out that you were off on some other journey. I wanted to move on too.

Vikas comes down and slowly walks towards Deepika.

VIKAS. To me wandering was life itself. I would not have stopped for anyone. Not even for life. Change tracks and move on. I travelled abroad and worked. Somewhere in one of those countries that need a small medical examination for all migrants, I found out. That somewhere, sometime, amidst the people whom I encountered, I had embraced the end of my life. Change tracks. Move on. Time to make a return journey. Went to Kamtipura, Falkland Street, Dharavi—all my usual haunts. They embraced me. I wanted to live and die there, where I felt loved. But then, one night I woke up with a dream. To kiss you once again. Goodbye. Of all the images that I have of all the people—I woke up with the vision of your face. I knew then what my destination was. But I looked into the mirror, and saw myself. I realized that it will soon be me who will move away by staying still.

DEEPIKA. I saw the lesions on you. I recognized your eyes.

VIKAS. You just picked up a pen and wrote, 'Patient admitted with Kaposi's Sarcoma.'

DEEPIKA. What did you expect? I am a doctor!

VIKAS. I will move. I will move towards you! I swore I will. Last stop. I couldn't abandon the journey without reaching my destination. I should have understood how difficult it must have been.

DEEPIKA. No. No, no, no! ... I couldn't let you see ... that I didn't love you. Any more. I couldn't hurt you. I just didn't love you ...

Silence.

DEEPIKA. It is my turn to wander.

Deepika exits.

Fade to:

SCENE IX

Deepika's cellphone starts to ring. We are now in the rehearsal of the play. Deepika is trying to placate an irate Mahesh and Amol. Through the screen we can see Amarinder dancing by himself while Shanti weeps and looks on.

MAHESH. You are a murderer!

AMOL. I am not a murderer!

MAHESH. Yes! I cannot stay in the same room as a murderer.

DEEPIKA. Why is he a murderer, Mr Kulkarni? Whom did he kill?

MAHESH. Goddess Saraswati! He keeps singing in his sleep 'Joi Shoshwati, Joi Shoshwati!' *(To Amol.)* Say 'Saraswati'. Come on. Say 'Saraswati'; then I will let you stay.

DEEPIKA. Go on, Mr Sengupta; just say it for him so we can sleep in peace.

AMOL. Joi Shoshwati! Jai Shoshwati! Give this buffalo some brains!

Mahesh starts pushing him out. Amol is pushed out screaming 'Joi Shoshwati!' Deepika tries to prevent Mahesh.

MAHESH. Answer your phone!

Deepika flips open her phone. Mahesh and Amol exit.

DEEPIKA. The answer is no! ... Oh. I am sorry. Who are you? ... *(She looks at her phone.)* Oh no! ... I am the wrong woman! ... No, No! You don't know me! ... No you don't have my number, this is not my phone! Whom do you want? ... Oh! Yes, of course. Today is her lucky day. She has got one man dancing for her in her room and another whistling on the phone ... What? Oh my God! No! Look I didn't mean that! I didn't! Let me explain!

Deepika rushes out.

Mahesh pops in and changes the room number on the door.

Amarinder waltzes in. A cellphone on the table begins to ring.

Shanti comes in to answer the phone.

Deepika rushes in.

DEEPIKA. Mrs Unnikrishnan! It's your husband on the phone.

SHANTI. Don't be silly. I haven't even answered it yet.

Before Deepika can say anything Amarinder butts in.

AMARINDER. What? She is married?

DEEPIKA. Yes, and I told her husband you were dancing in her room.

SHANTI. Oh no! *(Answering the phone.)* Look, I told you I am coming as soon as I get on the flight ...

AMARINDER *(to Deepika as she ducks to avoid him)*. Explain to me how you know she is talking to her husband!

DEEPIKA. She isn't.

SHANTI *(on phone)*. What? Oh no, no, no! I don't love you. And you are not my husband.

DEEPIKA. See.

AMARINDER. Explain to me how you know she has a husband.

SHANTI. And even if you are my husband I don't love you.

DEEPIKA. Because I am talking to her husband. *(On phone.)* Hang on a minute, will you?

Deepika dodges Amarinder and gets to Shanti.

AMARINDER. Then who is she talking to?

Deepika swaps phones.

DEEPIKA. Hello? The answer is no.

SHANTI. Hello? Why are you calling me at this hour?

AMARINDER *(puzzled)*. Hello?

SHANTI. No, I cannot bring Bombay Halwa for you. We are in the middle of a tsunami!

DEEPIKA. Why don't you just leave? Your flight will take off and you can forget all about me!

SHANTI. What man? Oh yes, the dancing man. Well he is—a man.

Amarinder is pleased with this.

DEEPIKA. But we don't know each other.

SHANTI. No, I haven't danced with him, yet.

DEEPIKA. No. No. That was so special. I shall always remember being stuck in the lift with you!

SHANTI. No. I will not dance for you.

AMARINDER. Good for you!

DEEPIKA. Just wait for a while. The storm will subside and you will take off into the sunrise.

SHANTI. It's all over. I don't want you with me. Find yourself another nurse.

AMARINDER. Good for you!

SHANTI. I have found myself someone to play doctor–nurse with!

AMARINDER. Good for me. Hurry up! I still have Viagra in my veins.

DEEPIKA. But why do you tell me now when you are leaving? You should have told me those three magic words when we were stuck together. Those three words that every woman wants to hear—'You turn me on.'

AMARINDER. Those are four words.

SHANTI. Who is counting?

DEEPIKA. So goodbye, Vishal.

SHANTI. Goodbye, husband.

They hang up.

SHANTI. Whee!

DEEPIKA. Whee!

SHANTI. Now I can be a real woman!

DEEPIKA. Now I can be a real hotel manager! No more attachments except on my Word files.

Mahesh and Amol come running in. They are fighting.

MAHESH. Me!

AMOL. No me! First me.

DEEPIKA. Gentlemen! Quiet! Now what is it?

AMOL. We want to say something to you.

DEEPIKA. What?

MAHESH *(kneeling)*. I love you!

AMOL *(kneeling)*. I love you!

Deepika gives an exaggerated expression of shock. They all get into a tableaux like at the end of a farce. After a moment.

SHANTI. Excellent.

They all clap with genuine enthusiasm.

AMOL. Three cheers for Shanti Venkatraman. Hip, Hip . . .

ALL. Hooray!

Shanti smiles and bows.

SHANTI. Thank you! Well . . . tomorrow we repor at the venue at 4 p.m. The play starts at 7. Shabana Azmi wil speak before that on cancer prevention and more facilities fo the hospice.

AMARINDER. Followed by a boring speech by the president of the club.

SHANTI. Yes, I forgot. And then, we are on. I am sure you will all do well.

Amol coughs. He gets out his handkerchief while the others are busy. Amol notices the blood on his handkerchief.

Amol's mood changes.

AMOL. And then, what happens after the play?

AMARINDER. We go home.

AMOL. He didn't write any other play, did he?

SHANTI. No, I am afraid not.

AMOL. So it will end tomorrow. And where do go?

AMARINDER. You don't have to worry. Your stay and medication has been taken care of.

Amarinder goes to Shanti.

Deepika instructs Mahesh on what to pack up.

AMARINDER. So are you really off to Chennai?

SHANTI. I don't know. My husband is waiting. Are you going to—go ahead with it?

AMARINDER. I might not.

Shanti moves away, akwardly.

Deepika, while leaving, stands face-to-face with Shanti.

Shanti avoids Amarinder and speaks to Deepka.

SHANTI. Thank you.

DEEPIKA. What for?

SHANTI. For doing this. It must be difficult for you to go through this.

DEEPIKA. Why does everyone feel it is difficult for me? It's not! As a matter of fact, I can't wait for this damn thing to get over.

AMOL. This 'damn thing' is all that I have left to do now.

DEEPIKA. Please! I am not interested. Mahesh!

AMOL. Not yet. We still need to rehearse something.

SHANTI. No, I think our next rehearsal will be onstage. Sleep well, all of you!

Amol begins to cough and now we hear the death rattle.

AMOL. I—don't want to—sleep.

DEEPIKA. Mahesh, get the stretcher.

AMOL *(grabbing Mahesh)*. No! Don't go. You need to rehearse the most.

DEEPIKA *(on the phone)*. Prepare the ICU now. And send Sawant with the stretcher to the lecture hall.

Deepika exits.

The others are around Amol. He lies down on the bed.

AMOL. Mahesh, you must learn to improvise. You know— Shanti—tell him to improvise.

SHANTI. You will be fine.

AMOL. You see, I don't want to die. But I don't want to cling on to life either ... Like Vikas did.

Vikas enters.

VIKAS. I wanted to let go. But I couldn't.

AMOL. Because Dr Dave forgot to kiss you goodbye? ... Will you tell Rose that I love her? That is why I don't want her to see me die.

AMARINDER. You will be fine, Amol. Hang in there.

AMOL. Will you?

AMARINDER. What?

AMOL. Hang in there?

AMARINDER *(nodding)*. I will. I will hang on.

AMOL. Maybe we can improvise that Mr Sengupta dies in the lobby drinking his Bloody Mary.

VIKAS. No, we can't. He will have to live.

AMOL. What if he can't?

VIKAS. He has no choice. It's a comedy, you see. In comedies, people don't die. That's why I wrote one.

Vikas looks at Deepika who has returned with a syringe.

Amol gives a very weak laugh. The death rattle stops.

VIKAS *(to Deepika)*. Just in time, as always.

Blackout.

Canned applause. A spotlight picks up Deepika.

Deepika speaks directly to the audience.

DEEPIKA. On behalf of Avedna, Cancer Research Hospital and Hospices, I thank you all for being here tonight. *Hotel Staylonger* is a comedy written by Vikas Tiwari. As you all know, he was a victim of cancer as a result of AIDS. He lived at our hospice for eight months. He died knowing that he was surrounded by people who cared. And that makes a difference.

Vikas enters.

Deepika throws a glance at him before continuing.

DEEPIKA. This play also shows, to all of us here, that all of us have a right to live as long as we can and to laugh at our own follies. Vikas Tiwari lives on through this play.

VIKAS. Goodbye, Deepika. I won't trouble you anymore.

DEEPIKA. On behalf of the department of senior doctors and the inmates of the hospice, as well as those who have been successfully treated in our hospital, I am proud to present *Hotel Staylonger*, a comedy in two acts. Directed by Shanti Venkatraman. Cast: Hotel Manager—Dr Deepika Dave; Kulkarni—Mahesh Tawade; Miss Unnikrishnan—Shanti Venkatraman; and Mr Sengupta by Amol—

She stops.

Silence.

DEEPIKA. Mr Sengupta does not appear onstage. He ... Well actually, Amol Ghosh, who was supposed to play Mr Sengupta, is—no longer with us. I—am sorry, I wanted to announce that he died last night but, we are presenting this play to you for your entertainment. A comedy. And like a person I once knew told me ... Nobody dies in a comedy. That's why people like them ... I just want the person to know that I love him very much.

VIKAS. Thank you. For your goodbye.

The farce music picks up as the lights cross-fade.

We have a fast forward of the first scene. Until it is Sengupta's cue.

MAHESH. Ah! I just saw a Sengputa run across the corridor, with a Bloody Mary in his hand!

AMARINDER *(yelling into the corridor)*. We are on the same flight tomorrow in the morning. Report at 0800!!

Fast forward to the scene where Amarinder falls down. Shanti screams.

SHANTI *(getting into the act)*. Oh no! He vanished before he could rob me of my youth!

Mahesh props him up on the bed.

MAHESH. He is dying.

SHANTI. He is dead, you mean.

MAHESH. No. No. He is dying.

SHANTI. He is alive, you mean.

MAHESH. Yes. If he is dying, he must be alive.

SHANTI. Somebody call a doctor!

Shanti runs to the door and yells.

SHANTI. Is there a doctor in this hotel? Doctor! Doctor!

Deepika appears.

SHANTI *(dragging her in).* Oh thank God, you are here.

Fast forward.

Shanti kisses Amarinder.

Vikas strums on his guitar.

Amarinder gets up.

AMARINDER. Darling! I can see again.

SHANTI. Oh my darling! I am so happy I could cry!

AMARINDER. Come on, let's complete the dance we started.

Amarinder begins to dance.

SHANTI. I can't! I can't!

Pause.

AMARINDER. Yes, you can.

Vikas starts to sing the song from Pyaasa. *Amol, who is with him, starts to hum the song.*

Shanti begins to waltz with Amarinder. Deepika and Vikas sing the duet standing apart but looking at each other.

Mahesh and Amol pretend to be playing an orchestra.

As Shanti and Amarinder waltz happily . . .

Fade out.

THE GIRL WHO TOUCHED THE STARS

A Radio Play

A Note on the Play

'While growing up, Bhavna has a dream. She want to fly to the moon and touch the stars. Bhavna's dreams do come rue—she is an astronaut and it is now 2025, and she is the first In ian woman to fly not to the moon but to Mars. But just afte take-off, the spacecraft explodes and she finds herself in space in dialogue with her childhood self.'

These were the words Mahesh Dattani used to desc be the play he wanted to write for BBC Radio 4. Well, how could i radio drama director like myself resist? Radio plays have the abil y to take you into a world of imagination. In radio the pictures re all in your head—and what pictures we could create with this olay! It was a superb piece to work on, with a wonderful cast, and tl e two days we spent rehearsing and recording the play were a joy.

The Girl Who Touched the Stars was inspired by the life of Kalpana Chawla, the first Indian woman in outer sp ce. Sadly, she never made it back to earth. But this isn't Kalpana' story—this is Bhavna's story, though with a twist in the tale. A d we relished telling the tale in the form of a radio play. It is a tribute to the bravery of Kalpana, but because we took the decisio to produce a fictional story it allowed us to create that dramatic c nflict between the older and young Bhavna, which then allowed a radiophonic conversation to be held in the middle of space. We co ld explore the dilemma that confronts a woman when she wants o hold on to reality and the present but finds herself drawn back into the past—when she feels a need to understand why she has beco ne the woman she is and why she was so eager to reach out and t the girl who touched the stars.

Tracey Neale
(Tracey Neale is Senior Producer, BBC adio Drama.)

The Girl Who Touched the Stars was first broadcast on 6 March 2007 at 2.15 p.m. on BBC Radio 4. The play was produced and directed by Tracey Neale.

Cast of the first production:

BHAVNA	Nina Wadia
YOUNG BHAVNA	Nita Mistry
MOTHER	Sakuntala Ramanee
FATHER	Amerjit Deu
GROUND CONTROL/REPORTER	Sam Dale
ASTRONAUT 1/JOURNALIST 3	John Dougall
ASTRONAUT 2/JOURNALIST 1	Anthony Glennon
JOURNALIST 2	Christine Kavanagh

Voices in the cockpit filtered through microphones. The voice from the base station is processed with an echo and sounds more disembodied, while the astronauts sound animated.

BASE STATION. Space shuttle, stand by for take-off.

ASTRONAUT 1. Well, lady and gentlemen. Wanna go to Mars?

ASTRONAUT 2. Oh my God! I forgot to water my ficus. Let me out!

Laughter.

BASE STATION. Space shuttle Mars 2025. Stand by for take-off. You have seven seconds before countdown.

BHAVNA. Okay, boys. Time to leave this planet.

ASTRONAUT 1 *(speaking into a microphone).* Standing by for take-off.

A lullaby in Hindi begins. A soft female voice. It could be 'Chanda Mama'.

The countdown begins under the song. 10-9-8-7-6-5-4-3-2-1-0. the sound of the rocket taking off drowns out the lullaby. Fade out.

Credits.

Flashbulbs going off at random moments during the scene as Bhavna takes questions from the media.

JOURNALIST 1. Bhavna, what are you thinking of at this moment?

BHAVNA. I need to use the loo.

Laughter.

BHAVNA. It will be a while before I use a regular loo. When I come back, I will discover the joy of watching the water go

57

right down the commode, and marvel at that simple truth that we all take for granted—that everything goes down. That when you flush a toilet, the water won't dance in front of your face.

Laughter.

JOURNALIST 2. What do you have to say to the rest of the women of your country?

BHAVNA. I really have nothing to say to them . . . Really!

JOURNALIST 2. Bhavna, you are the only Indian woman to go to Mars. There are millions of women in your country watching you at this very moment.

BHAVNA. Are they? *(Thinking about it.)* All I can say is that I am happy to be where I am. And happy to be going where I am going. I know that not everyone is as blessed as I am, but if at all you are at some place you don't want to be, or if you want to go somewhere you can't . . . at least dream. Who knows, this might well be a dream and I might wake up to find myself in a place that makes me unhappy. But if this is a dream, I am thankful I have it.

JOURNALIST 3. How important a role do your parents have in your success?

The lullaby again. At the same time we hear Bhavna's father: 'Bhavna! Don't hide! Okay, I promise you may marry the man of your choice when you grow up, okay?'

BHAVNA. I wouldn't be here without help from my parents.

JOURNALIST 1. Who would you like to thank today at this moment?

BHAVNA. God.

JOURNALIST 2. Are you a religious person?

BHAVNA. I thank God that being a woman or an Indian has nothing to do with my journey . . .

Fade in: Bhavna's mother hums the lullaby. We hear the shuttle taking off. The shuttle fades out but the humming continues.

The astronauts speak through their communication system, and so their voices sound filtered.

ASTRONAUT 1. Got it. Do you think it will stay?

BHAVNA. A bit gross, but . . . always kept it handy, never used it—until now. Who would have thought? In 2025?

ASTRONAUT 1 *(to Base Station)*. Base. Heat shield in place.

BASE STATION. Oh great. You sure everything is okay?

BHAVNA. Trillions of dollars of NASA technology, saved by Elmer's glue and a Swiss knife.

The lullaby continues for a few seconds before fading out as an explosion far away somewhere. Almost like serial bombs going off. Followed by a deathly silence.

BHAVNA. How did you get here?

YOUNG BHAVNA. Who are you?

BHAVNA. I am your future. No . . . No. Let me tell you who you are.

YOUNG BHAVNA. I know who I am. But . . . where am I? I was daydreaming in school and I heard you call my name. Why did you call my name and why do you say you are my future?

BHAVNA. I am your future because you are gone. You are my past.

YOUNG BHAVNA. Are you suggesting that I don't exist except in your imagination?

BHAVNA. Yes. Otherwise you wouldn't show up here.

YOUNG BHAVNA. And where are we?

BHAVNA *(thinking about it)*. I—I don't know.

YOUNG BHAVNA *(laughing)*. And you call me unreal. Let me explain how I got here, wherever here is . . . I was watching you. Then you got into your suit and—began to think about me . . .

The countdown, again, as if in another place: '6-5-4-3-2-1-0. Take-off.' Followed by the firing of engines. Cheers from her colleagues inside the spaceship.

BHAVNA. At least we have a fix on reality now.

YOUNG BHAVNA. Do we?

Sound of the rocket taking off. Deafening at first, but it fades away.

BHAVNA. Yes . . . Did you see that?

YOUNG BHAVNA. Oh that! I dream about spaceships all the time.

BHAVNA. That is the real moment and we are inside my head right now.

YOUNG BHAVNA. Or mine. And that image is what I am thinking of now. Maybe there is another image of me somewhere which is the real one.

A cry of crickets. A television set in the background. A woman's voice calls in the distance: 'Bhavna-a-a! Come for dinner you star-gazing girl! Bhavna-a-a!'

YOUNG BHAVNA. There. That's the real moment. That's where we are.

BHAVNA. No. That's done and over with. That's the past.

YOUNG BHAVNA. It is not. It is 2006 and I am dreaming of going out into space.

BHAVNA. It is 2025 and you are with me. Wherever I am.

Pause.

YOUNG BHAVNA. I want to find out whether my dreams do come true.

BHAVNA. And what is your dream?

YOUNG BHAVNA. I want to walk on the moon.

Bhavna laughs at this.

BHAVNA. On the moon? Did you say the moon?

YOUNG BHAVNA. What is so funny about that?

BHAVNA. I know you are unreal! To think I doubted my existence. The moon!

YOUNG BHAVNA. What is wrong with that? I want to be the first woman on the moon.

BHAVNA. You are thinking of going where only men have been before. I am going where no man has gone. To Mars.

YOUNG BHAVNA. Is that where you are going?

BHAVNA. You don't watch the news. You must be unreal.

A TV news reporter: 'According to top NASA scientist Dr Lee Hwang, this trip is possible because of the breakthrough in spacesuit material. Apart from the successful application of hydrogen slush fuel, that is. Temperatures in Mars can vary from 20°C at the equator but . . .'

YOUNG BHAVNA. Not so fast. I am not convinced . . . You are not wearing your suit.

BHAVNA. What does it matter? I will go back to wearing my suit. Clearly this is not the time to think of you.

Pause.

BHAVNA. You said you had something to ask me. *(Thinking about it.)* You actually interrupted my thought. I was thinking of those journalists when suddenly I heard your voice . . . You wanted to know something. What is it? What's your question?

YOUNG BHAVNA. You answered it. Whether you do exist. Whether it really will happen.

Bhavna thinks about it.

BHAVNA. It might. I don't know. I haven't done it yet. I'll come back to tell you about it.

Pause.

YOUNG BHAVNA. I have an awful feeling.

BHAVNA. I am sure you do. We all have them.

YOUNG BHAVNA. Maybe you are dead.

Pause.

BHAVNA. No. I can't be dead.

YOUNG BHAVNA. How can you rule that out? What if that image is wrong? Maybe you are at this moment blown to pieces, with your arms, your legs, your torso flying in different directions, and some part of you—maybe a part of your brain—is thinking of me.

BHAVNA. It can't be. I would remember, wouldn't I?

YOUNG BHAVNA. What if your brain is smashed to a thousand different pieces and some other part of your brain remembers your death and this part of you—the part that remembers me—doesn't remember anything else!

BHAVNA. You were never such a pessimist. I always remember you being so positive.

YOUNG BHAVNA. I am. Which means I could be right.

BHAVNA. What? Are you suggesting that I am dead? If I died, you wouldn't exist either. So maybe we are both dead. Is that what you are saying?

YOUNG BHAVNA. I never said that. I know somehow that I stayed alive.

BHAVNA. To become me.

YOUNG BHAVNA. I don't know. I don't know.

BHAVNA. I don't understand you. You chose the wrong moment to meet me. Before things have happened. That is why I feel I am the one in charge. I have every reason to remember you—I . . .

The explosion is heard once again, except it seems closer now.

BHAVNA. What is that?

YOUNG BHAVNA. Your death?

BHAVNA. I don't remember that!

YOUNG BHAVNA. Like I said, this is just a fragment of your brain that remembers me.

BHAVNA. It's not true.

YOUNG BHAVNA. Those images never lie! Don't you see? That's what gives us a fix on reality. Those images are real!

BHAVNA. Look at it closely. It only shows one piece, it looks like a reflector.

YOUNG BHAVNA. Maybe it is now, but—

BHAVNA *(controlling her fluster)*. That's to be expected, when the shuttle leaves the atmosphere or enters it. There's bound to be some friction and sometimes parts are known to come off. It doesn't mean I didn't return. In fact—it doesn't mean I have been there.

Pause.

BHAVNA. Maybe I am on my way. You see, the images may be real but we still don't know the truth. Because it doesn't give us the time. Or the right sequence.

YOUNG BHAVNA. I think it's telling us something, though.

BHAVNA. Something I have always believed in. That it doesn't matter. All that matters is whether I lived my dream.

YOUNG BHAVNA. That is what I want to know.

BHAVNA. And I don't have the answer to that.

YOUNG BHAVNA. But that is what I want to know from you!

BHAVNA. I want to know that from you.

YOUNG BHAVNA. That's absurd! How would I know? You can't look backwards to answer that.

BHAVNA. You can. And I am. The more I think of it, I know the moment I am in.

Loud cheers. The news reporter can barely contain his excitement: 'There they are, waving to the cameras as they enter the shuttle that will take them to their ship ... Michael Waterman, Lou Miles, Bhavna Patel ...'

YOUNG BHAVNA. But that is exactly how I dream it will be!

BHAVNA. It's all done. I rebelled, I went to NASA against all odds, took all the jibes, passed all the tests, passed the physicals and finally, my dream comes true. I am taking a journey that no human from this planet has taken. It is the biggest moment of my life and—I think of you. Because I have a doubt. *(Trying to find the words.)* Is this really what I want? Is this my dream?

We are back with the crickets and Bhavna's mother shouting: 'Bhavna-a-a! Shut that window, you're letting in all the mosquitoes! Bhavna-a-a!'

YOUNG BHAVNA. Yes, it is! Oh God! It's come true! I will get out there! I will break away! I will—touch the stars! Nothing else will do for me. I want to go out there.

Crickets. Bhavna responds to her mother: 'Coming!'

YOUNG BHAVNA. Yes! It is what I really want to do. How can you even doubt it?

Pause.

BHAVNA. How old are you?

YOUNG BHAVNA. What a question to ask? How old—I don't know.

BHAVNA. Please, this is important.

YOUNG BHAVNA. Nine, twelve, fifteen—oh, I don't know these things. Time is vague when you are not in real space. You yourself said that about those images. It's not that they don't tell you their time, it's just that we don't understand it in that way.

Bhavna thinks for a while.

BHAVNA. All right. Since time is vague for us. Let me go deeper.

YOUNG BHAVNA. Deeper where?

BHAVNA. Deeper into your thoughts. That is the only real space for us right now. So that is where I will have to look for answers.

YOUNG BHAVNA. Might as well go into the black hole. I don't think I can go any deeper than this.

BHAVNA. It's very simple. Just think.

YOUNG BHAVNA. Think of what?

BHAVNA. Think of your father.

YOUNG BHAVNA. Why?

BHAVNA. Can you do that for me, please?

YOUNG BHAVNA. I want to know why?

BHAVNA. I just want to know . . . I want to know whether this is what I want or whether it is—someone else's dream.

YOUNG BHAVNA. This is what I want!

BHAVNA. That's not good enough for me. Please. Just think of him.

YOUNG BHAVNA. Are you suggesting that it is my father who wants me to go to the moon?

BHAVNA. I don't know—

YOUNG BHAVNA. I can tell you right away that's not true. Don't you remember? Or maybe I shouldn't ask that question ever. Father never wanted me to study further. He wanted me to marry his best friend's son when I am twenty-two and live in Bhuj for the rest of my life! How can you even think that this was his dream? Do you see that image? You know it doesn't lie. That's me dreaming of touching the stars.

BHAVNA. You know, there is another thing about those images. They don't tell you why. That is why I need to ask you that. Why did you want to fly to the moon?

YOUNG BHAVNA *(sarcastic)*. Because it's there!

BHAVNA. There are two things I want of you and you don't do either. And that leads me to believe I should persist with you. One, you don't want to think of your father and two, you don't want to think of why you want to go to the moon.

YOUNG BHAVNA *(thinking of it)*. Really?

BHAVNA. Really.

YOUNG BHAVNA. So if I think of my father, you feel we will get somewhere?

BHAVNA. Yes. Somewhere. If we get a fix on space we will get a fix on time as well. We have spent enough time *(Laughing over the word 'time'.)* speculating whose time we are in. Now we can spend some space on that question. Whose space are we in? Tell me the space, don't tell me the time. Tell me the space. Tell me the space. Tell me the space . . .

YOUNG BHAVNA *(under Bhavna's 'Tell me the space').* I am trying, I am trying.

> *Bhavna goes on with 'Tell me the space' while the young Bhavna goes on saying, 'I am trying.'*

> *A car drives out of a garage.*

YOUNG BHAVNA. Daddy!

> *The man is lost in a different space. Distant, but at the same time, intrusive.*

FATHER. Hurry up, Bhavna! You will miss the bus and I will have to take you.

YOUNG BHAVNA. Coming, Daddy! I can't find my maths book!

FATHER. Come on!

YOUNG BHAVNA. Is this what you wanted?

> *A honk.*

FATHER. Bhavna!

YOUNG BHAVNA. He is waiting. I have to go!

BHAVNA. No, don't go. There is something I have to tell you.

YOUNG BHAVNA. Can't it wait? What do you want to do now? You told me to think of him and I did! Sorry, have to rush!

BHAVNA. I just had a doubt. You don't know yet! Can't you think of another time? Some time earlier?

YOUNG BHAVNA *(trying to break free).* Don't be silly! You know that time doesn't work that way for us! I can't stop my thoughts now. Let me go! I am running late for school.

> *Activity inside as Bhavna's mother comes to her.*

MOTHER. Bhavna, you left your maths book under your pillow! How can you leave it there?

A couple of honks from the car.

MOTHER. She's coming! *(To young Bhavna.)* Quickly, oh child, put the book in your bag or you will lose it! Now go! Go!

FATHER. Bhavna, I am leaving! Take a rickshaw and go to school.

BHAVNA. Let him go! I want to talk to you.

YOUNG BHAVNA. Let go of my arm!

An impatient honk.

MOTHER *(shouting to the man).* She is ready! Wait! *(To young Bhavna.)* Go!

BHAVNA. Bhavna! He didn't want you!

The young Bhavna stops as she hears this. Her mother escorts her to the door.

MOTHER. This girl is always dreaming, dreaming, dreaming. My head is going round just worrying about you. Now go!

The door slams. We are now inside a moving car. Some traffic on the road.

FATHER. Bhavna, I got a call from your principal . . . Is it true?

No response. They drive.

FATHER. You shouldn't be climbing trees. If you want mangoes, buy them from the store.

YOUNG BHAVNA. I don't climb the tree for the mangoes!

FATHER. Then why do you skip class and climb trees?

No response.

YOUNG BHAVNA. You didn't want me.

FATHER *(laughing).* And what put that thought in your head?

YOUNG BHAVNA. I had a brother, didn't I?

The car comes to a halt.

YOUNG BHAVNA. And you told him he could be a pilot. You told him you would like him to be a pilot. And you never told me any such thing!

FATHER. Are you all right?

The young Bhavna gets out of the car.

YOUNG BHAVNA. Am I right?

Bhavna's father gets out of the car.

FATHER. I don't know what you are thinking. But it wasn't that way at all.

Pause.

YOUNG BHAVNA. I am sorry. It's okay. I will walk to school. You go ahead, Daddy. It's getting late for you.

FATHER. Now come straight home from school. Bye ... And Bhavna, no more climbing trees. Okay?

Bhavna's father shuts his car door and drives away even as young Bhavna speaks.

YOUNG BHAVNA. Why did you say that?

BHAVNA. You know. You know exactly what I mean.

YOUNG BHAVNA. No, I don't. I don't know what you mean!

BHAVNA. Don't pretend. The bit about your father telling his son to be a pilot? Where did that come from if you don't know what I am talking about?

YOUNG BHAVNA. What? That I had a brother who died?

BHAVNA. No. Didn't you hear what he said? It wasn't that at all.

YOUNG BHAVNA. I shouldn't listen to you. Maybe you are brain dead. Lack of oxygen or something.

BHAVNA. You don't take me seriously, do you?

YOUNG BHAVNA. If I took you seriously, I would feel that doing what I want to do is not going to make me happy.

BHAVNA. I never said that—

YOUNG BHAVNA. But you give me the impression. Come on. You are on your way to bloody Mars. It's more than what I dream of. And here you are, talking to me instead.

BHAVNA. I forget. I forget how impulsive you are. And how reflective I am.

YOUNG BHAVNA. Coming back to what you said. So what if I had a brother who didn't survive?

Bhavna's mother sings her lullaby.

BHAVNA. Why is she still lingering over here?

Bhavna's mother is humming a song from an old Hindi film, a lullaby for a little boy.

YOUNG BHAVNA. There must be a reason. Neither of us thought of her. Yet she is there. She refuses to go away. *(To Bhavna.)* Are you dodging my question?

BHAVNA. No. You won't believe me if I tell you. That is why subconsciously I have been thinking of mother. She has to tell you. I can't. It doesn't seem right.

YOUNG BHAVNA. Why?

BHAVNA. It just doesn't seem right. There are things that happened, and you have to make them exist in your memory. I am just a thought, so it won't be real to tell you. Besides I want to be sure too.

YOUNG BHAVNA. So what do you want me to do now?

BHAVNA. We are thinking of Mother. So concentrate on her. Something will happen.

Bhavna's mother continues to hum the song.

YOUNG BHAVNA. We are both thinking of her and yet nothing seems to happen.

BHAVNA. I am not thinking of her.

YOUNG BHAVNA. Of course you are. You are talking of her.

BHAVNA. It's not the same thing. This is of no use to me. I want to know your dreams! I can only do that if you think and face the truth!

YOUNG BHAVNA. You want me to spill out my thoughts to you so that you can reflect, analyse, work things out.

BHAVNA. Yes.

YOUNG BHAVNA. I want exactly that of you.

BHAVNA. I am sorry. I treat you like you are just a result of my thoughts. But you lived too—

YOUNG BHAVNA. I live. *Live*. Present moment.

BHAVNA. Sorry, sorry. You live too.

YOUNG BHAVNA. It's unfair! It's unfair to me that you can dig, probe, ferret out information, whereas I can't even know from you whether I will go to the moon or not.

BHAVNA. I think you did.

YOUNG BHAVNA. What?

BHAVNA. Go to the moon.

YOUNG BHAVNA. That's no use! It's the same as me saying 'I think I will go to the moon.'

BHAVNA. You think you will. And I think you did. That is the only real thing we can fix now. That and the truth.

YOUNG BHAVNA. I—I don't want to know the past. I want to know the future.

BHAVNA. I love you. No matter what you did or what was done to you, I will always be thankful I have you ... Bhavna, listen to that lullaby she is singing.

YOUNG BHAVNA. I am listening.

BHAVNA. Can you tell?

YOUNG BHAVNA. What?

BHAVNA. I can see it now. You can't, but I can.

YOUNG BHAVNA. What is it about the lullaby?

The singing stops.

Footsteps running indoors and slamming the door.

YOUNG BHAVNA. Do you remember that?

BHAVNA. Was it the same day? I really can't ...

YOUNG BHAVNA. That's the day, all right. I had a stomach ache the whole day. I thought I would get away from class and get away from the punishment of not having done my homework.

BHAVNA. I felt different from the rest.

YOUNG BHAVNA. I climbed the tree.

BHAVNA. It was my escape from ugliness.

YOUNG BHAVNA. I thought I was going to throw up.

BHAVNA. It was better than that.

YOUNG BHAVNA. They were all there at break. The girls who called me a tomboy. The boys. They were there under the tree, opening their lunch boxes.

BHAVNA. Almost as if I was proving something.

YOUNG BHAVNA. I spilt out with a vengeance. Why was I terrified? Why was I ashamed? That shame took away my moment of triumph. I proved myself, on top of somebody's head. In someone's lunch box. They all knew I was a woman and they all knew I could climb that tree.

BHAVNA. I became a woman, standing on the highest branch of the tallest mango tree in my school yard. Looking down at the world.

YOUNG BHAVNA. But I didn't have any of those thoughts when it happened! All I could think of was Mummy. I wanted to go home! Away from those disgusted faces staring at me. I—I couldn't come down till the bell rang and they had to go back to class. The teacher stood there, the poor man didn't know what to do. His face went as red as . . . I fell down and ran. I went straight home and—

Again, the sound of footsteps running indoors and the slamming of the door.

YOUNG BHAVNA. Mummy!

MOTHER. What is it? Bhavna, what happened?

YOUNG BHAVNA. I am bleeding. You never told me! I thought it won't happen so soon.

MOTHER. It's okay. It's okay. These things happen sooner than you expect. Come with me.

YOUNG BHAVNA. It's okay. I feel better. I just won't go back to school.

MOTHER. Take a bath now. You can stay at home today. I will make you some kheer.

YOUNG BHAVNA. I don't want to go to that school again! Never!

MOTHER. I understand. Take some rest today and you will feel better tomorrow.

YOUNG BHAVNA. I am not going there tomorrow or ever.

MOTHER. All girls go through this. But every girl does not stop going to school because of that.

YOUNG BHAVNA. I am different.

MOTHER. Why are you different?

YOUNG BHAVNA. They don't want me in school and you never wanted me. You tried to get rid of me.

MOTHER. Now go inside.

Footsteps fading away.

BHAVNA. That's all I need to know. It's true. I am not just imagining things.

YOUNG BHAVNA. I want to know more! How dare you drag me into your thoughts?

BHAVNA. You will know more. It's clear. You are my dream. At one point I was yours but that's all over!

YOUNG BHAVNA. It's not! It will never be over! Think. Think of him! I want to see him.

BHAVNA. Turn around! There he is! Look!

Bhavna's mother resumes humming the lullaby, now even louder.

BHAVNA. He is flooding my thoughts.

The young Bhavna gives a gasp which is stifled.

BHAVNA. Shh!

YOUNG BHAVNA. This is too long ago. She is expecting a child.

BHAVNA. You. Me. But the lullaby.

YOUNG BHAVNA. Yes. I understand. It is to a baby boy.

The singing continues.

FATHER. Shh!!

YOUNG BHAVNA. I asked you to show me the future! Not the past. Please! Take him away.

BHAVNA. It doesn't work that way. Future. Past. It's all the same now. As random as our thoughts.

FATHER. Is everything all right?

MOTHER *(stops her humming to answer him and then resumes)*. Yes. Our son is all right. The doctor said he is fine.

FATHER. I wish I could stay. I will give up this job one day, you see. Or maybe you can join me in Dubai. Life is hard there. But we will be together.

YOUNG BHAVNA. He was never there. That thought was completely pointless. Why bring that up?

BHAVNA. Maybe it had a point. I can't control those images. So now I can ask you that question again. Did you really want to go to the moon?

The song fades out.

Camera clicks.

JOURNALIST 1. So what are you thinking of right now, Mr Patel?

FATHER. I am thinking of the responsibility on my daughter as the first Indian woman to step on the moon. The responsibility of making this a successful space mission that will pave the way for future generations of Indians who have similar aspirations.

JOURNALIST 2. Do you believe in God?

FATHER. Yes. I most certainly do. There is a God and I do believe in His powers.

JOURNALIST 2. Is there anything you would like to say to the people of your country?

FATHER. Well, I just want to say that I am proud to be Bhavna's father and proud to be an Indian. And I am proud to be from Nadiad, a small town in Gujarat.

Applause.

FATHER. Wait! I want to speak to her! I want to tell my daughter . . .

YOUNG BHAVNA. Why do I have to deal with the past?

BHAVNA. Because . . . if you really want to know, you cannot lie to yourself . . . I am still trying.

YOUNG BHAVNA. You are right. I am dead. So are you.

BHAVNA. Mother is gone too. Only he remains.

FATHER. I loved you. I really did. I loved you. Till the very—end. I loved you.

BHAVNA. But I didn't.

YOUNG BHAVNA. Don't talk to him!

Footsteps approaching.

YOUNG BHAVNA. I don't want to talk to him!

BHAVNA. But I do.

FATHER. Bhavna!

BHAVNA. Hello, Father.

FATHER. Bhavna! They told me you were . . .

BHAVNA. Dead?

FATHER. Yes. I wanted to talk to you before you took off, but they couldn't connect me and then—they gave me the news . . . Where am I?

BHAVNA. In my thoughts.

FATHER. What a strange place to be in.

BHAVNA. Yes. I wanted to talk to her but I find you.

FATHER. Who is she?

YOUNG BHAVNA. Don't you remember me?

FATHER. Do I know you?

YOUNG BHAVNA. No . . . You don't.

FATHER. Bhavna, what is this girl talking about?

YOUNG BHAVNA. I am your daughter.

FATHER. That's not true.

A baby's wail approaching.

MOTHER. Shh! Shh! Look, Daddy is home. You want to play with Daddy?

YOUNG BHAVNA. Who is that?

FATHER. Shh! My son isn't feeling too well. *(Calling out.)* Bhuvan!

MOTHER. He has been crying all night.

FATHER. Give him to me.

Bhavna's father hums the lullaby while her mother speaks.

MOTHER. Our son. You know, your father told me he would have me thrown out of the house if I did not give him a grandson . . .

FATHER. What does it matter? You have given me a son.

MOTHER. Give him to me. I need to change his diaper.

FATHER. I am quitting my job to spend more time with you and our son—

MOTHER. No. No. Please, don't do that! Please!

FATHER. No, let me hold him . . . I will change his—

MOTHER. Oh God! I am sorry! I am sorry!

YOUNG BHAVNA. That wasn't my brother. That was me.

MOTHER *(running to Bhavna)*. I am sorry, Bhavna. But you are all I have.

YOUNG BHAVNA. I am all you have because you couldn't have anyone else.

FATHER. I didn't know. She tricked me. For five years.

BHAVNA. That is not true. You knew. You pretended you had a son. Of course you knew all along!

MOTHER. But I loved you. I was scared.

FATHER. It didn't matter. When I found out.

A little girl's laughter.

FATHER. That is my son!

The little girl laughs. The father and mother join in.

MOTHER. Look at the stars! He wants to touch the stars!

FATHER. When Bhuvan grows up, he will become a pilot and fly near the moon!

YOUNG BHAVNA. And when I wore a skirt for the first time, you never told me that I will go to the moon.

FATHER. I did! I did educate you, I did encourage you to study, didn't I?

YOUNG BHAVNA. Tell me father. If you had known . . . If mother had told you the truth, that the doctors said that she will have a healthy girl . . . You would have—

FATHER. No!

YOUNG BHAVNA.—killed me.

The mother sings a lullaby: 'Chanda Mama'.

BHAVNA. I walked on it, Mummy. The moon. Not what I imagined it to be, but then . . . It sort of takes away a part of you. The part that believes in Chanda Mama. Uncle Moon.

The mother continues to sing.

BHAVNA. It takes away all that, but . . . it puts in something else. You look at things, in a special way. You look at yourself . . . It wasn't the moon, really, that made me think in that special way. It was the earth.

YOUNG BHAVNA. Far away. So far away from my bedroom. The earth looked exactly like how I looked at the moon when I was a child. It made me a child again. To be able to look at earth with the same wonderment with which I looked at the moon when I was a child. The earth looked beautiful. Uncle Earth. That is what I thought of when I saw it from there.

BHAVNA. Out there. Somewhere no Indian woman has ever been. Getting to the moon was no longer a dream. But then I was dreaming again, about being a part of the earth. The same magic that I believed in about the moon, I began to see it in my own world! How lucky I was to belong to that magical planet.

YOUNG BHAVNA. Where nothing weighed you down. Not even the weight of your pain.

BHAVNA. Thank you for talking to me, Bhavna. At this moment, when I thought of you. My last thought. I am burning; but it is no longer hell. My body is torn apart; but I no longer feel pain. My blood once again spills on the earth. The earth is one big mango tree and I am on top of it. I never have to come down again.

YOUNG BHAVNA. I love you.

BHAVNA. And you are the only person I love.

The humming of the lullaby continues even as Bhavna's mother speaks.

MOTHER. Go, Bhavna! Set yourself free! Go where I could never go!

We hear a series of explosions, quite close now.

The humming fades out.

THIRTY DAYS IN SEPTEMBER

A Stage Play in Three Acts

A Note on the Play

My friend Protima Bedi once told me that when she first saw the land on which Nrityagram now stands, it whispered to her that it wanted to be a dance village.

Such is the stuff of dreams and Protima's wonderful, soaring imagination!

The plays closest to my heart, that have transformed and changed me in some way, happen in somewhat the same manner. They seem to have a voice of their own, a voice that *demands* that they be done . . . and I have no choice.

But then the oddest thing happens! The universe *does* conspire to make it so. (Together, of course, with a team of very hard-working actors, artists and technicians, plus the generous support of enlightened sponsors like the Tatas, who often support me on the strength of my passion!)

In August 2000, when I was shooting for *Monsoon Wedding* in Delhi, Mahesh met me and told me over a cup of coffee, that he had been commissioned by RAHI to write a play on child sexual abuse and would like me to consider producing it. I agreed almost immediately. It was the first time that I committed to doing a play, without even seeing an outline of the script! But RAHI's commitment, Mahesh's integrity and my own response to the subject, left me in no doubt that this was a play I had to do! My only condition was that the play should work first and foremost as a piece of theatre, that the issues addressed should be organic to the plot and the message subliminal.

The 'tripartite' talks that followed as the script began to take shape, between RAHI, Mahesh and me, were probably one of the most interesting aspects of the project. With RAHI striving to ensure authenticity (every survivor and psychologist who has seen the play is amazed by its veracity!), to me insisting on it being a strong stand-alone piece of dramatic work and Mahesh struggling to walk the delicate tightrope between both, while interviewing over a dozen survivors and moulding their stories to provide a framework of truthfulness for our tale, life was fraught with frantic phone calls and flying emails!

And then the actors moved in. Rehearsals, workshops and the individual inputs of the actors reshaped the material further and a slightly different avatar of the play was born.

The play turned out to be a liberating and learning experience for everyone involved. Especially for the actors, who had to delve deep into unexplored areas of themselves in order to connect truthfully with the material of the play, through intense workshops that often left them shaken and not a little disturbed. Especially for the actors who played the abuser—first Darshan Jariwala and later Amar Talwar—it was a process that took them into the heart of darkness! Their reward was the passionate dislike they evoked in the audience for their superb portrayals!

If rehearsing the play was a journey of discovery, the performance was a revelation! A dark piece, albeit powerful and immensely moving, its commercial success and critical acclaim took us all by surprise. We were amazed at the depth of emotion and strong outrage it evoked in audiences across the world from varied cities in India to Colombo (where we performed for an audience of over 900 to a five-minute standing ovation!) to the US and Malaysia (where the image of young Malay girls in their headdresses, watching wide-eyed, will never leave me).

Thirty Days in September has touched hearts and consciences everywhere. Sensitive and powerful without ever offending sensibilities, it manages to bring home the horror and the pain within the framework of a very identifiable mother–daughter relationship. (On a personal level, *that* was quite poignant for me as well, because *Thirty Days in September* was the first time I played 'Ma' on stage, to both my daughters, Neha and Ira, who played the title role at different times.)

After every performance, women have come backstage with their own traumatic stories writ large on their faces, grateful for the catharsis the play offers, but even more, I think, for the expiation of their own guilt which they have carried as a heavy burden for so long. Meeting them, alone, has made the play worthwhile. For through it, they believe, their silent screams have finally been heard.

To do plays moored in a living social context provides a fulfilment of its own. And to do those which deal with subjects that simmer dangerously below the surface of our consciousness, even if the seeing of them discomforts us, is surely one of the aims of theatre.

Peter Brooks once said that if a play did not provoke and disturb the audience, it wasn't worth doing.

I don't think there could be a better way to put it.

Lillete Dubey

(Lillete Dubey is a well-known theatre personality and stage director. She has directed Dattani's Dance Like a Man, On a Muggy Night in Mumbai, Thirty Days in September *and* Brief Candle.*)*

Thirty Days in September was first performed at the Prithvi Theatre, Mumbai, on 31 May 2001 with the following cast:

MALA	Nandana Sen
SHANTA	Lillete Dubey
THE MAN	Darshan Jariwala
DEEPAK	Joy Sengupta

Producer–Director	Lillete Dubey
Light Design	Lynne Fernandez
Set Design	Bhola Sharma
Vocals	Ila Arun
Original Music	Mahesh Tinaikar
Sound	Nupur Goel
Puppet Design	Ramdas Pandhye

In subsequent performances of the play, the part of Mala was played by Neha Dubey and Ira Dubey. The Man was played by Amar Talwar.

The play was commissioned by RAHI, a support group for women survivors of incest. RAHI was supported by the John D. and Catherine T. MacArthur Foundation.

ACT I

The stage is divided into four acting areas. All the action moves without any set changes between scenes.

The first area has a comfortable chair and a simple table with magazines and a double seater. The chair is reserved for the counsellor whom we never see.

The second area, occupying the central portion of the stage, is the living room of Shanta and Mala's home in a suburb of Delhi. The dominant feature is a large picture of Shri Krishna. The furniture is basic and minimal, almost as if this is just a point of transition rather than a room where the family would meet and receive people.

The third area is the pooja room which is perhaps behind a scrim so that it is visible only when required. The scrim will go up in the last scene as specified.

The fourth acting area is the most flexible, representing several locations—a party house, two restaurants, Deepak's home. Since this area is more representational, it would suffice to have four cubes that could be configured by the actors before the required scene, in full view of the audience.

During Mala's taped conversation, we see the back of a life-sized doll of a seven-year-old girl propped up on a chair. During the first conversation we only see the back of the head. With every subsequent taped conversation, we see more of the profile. We only see the doll's full face after Deepak's taped conversation.

Optional: During Mala's taped conversation, the director could choose to have a video projection of Mala, but it is important that the image is disjointed from her conversation. The video should focus on close-ups and/or her body language with the idea of providing a contrast to Mala's confidence and clarity after four years as seen in the sessions with the counsellor.

The lights come up on Mala seated at the counsellor's desk. This Mala is more at peace with herself. She has taken a journey and has arrived somewhere, psychologically. This could be reflected in her easy manner or body language.

Mala talks to the imagined counsellor in the single seater opposite her. She does not talk to the audience. There is a tape recorder on the table, but she is not self-conscious about the recording.

MALA. Mala Khatri. February 2004 ... *(Listening to the counsellor.)* Why not? ... I do not hesitate to use my real name now. Let people know. There's nothing to hide. Not for me. After all, it is he who must hide. He should change his name, not me. It is he who must avoid being recognized. In people's homes, at parties, hopefully even on the streets. He should look the other way when someone spots him anywhere on this planet. And I can make that happen. I have the power to do that now. If I use my real name ... *(Sighing, thinking about it almost as if it were a pleasant memory.)* I wish he were here now, so I could see his face when I tell him I have nothing to hide. Because I know it wasn't my fault ... Now. I know now.

Pause.

MALA *(saying it with a growing sense of joy).* But what is the point? He is dead. Today. February the 29th. He is dead. Today.

Fade to black. Mala's voice on tape plays in the blackout. This voice of Mala's is more unsure and a great deal more nervous.

MALA. I—I don't know how to begin ... Today is the 30th of September ... 2001, and my name is ... I don't think I want to say my name ... I am sorry. I hope that is okay with you ... I am unsure about this ... and a lot of other things. But this ... This is the first time you see that I ... *(After a long pause, where we do hear her breathing.)* I know it is all my fault really ... It must be. I must have asked for it ... Somehow, I just seem to be made for it. Maybe I was born that way, maybe ... This is what I am meant for. It's not anybody's fault, except my own. Sometimes I wish that my mother ... *(It gets to be difficult for her.)* I am sorry but ... I can only tell you more if you turn this thing off.

The tape continues to hiss for a while.

Fade in. Music. The lights fade in on Shanta, Mala's mother, in the prayer room. Shanta is singing softly to herself while she rings a bell. The music fades out. Late evening.

Shanta offers some flowers and picks up the bell once again while she sings.

SHANTA *(singing).* 'Mere to Giridhar Gopal, doosro na koi, mere to Giridhar Gopal, doosro na koi ...'

The doorbell rings.

Shanta stops singing, puts the bell down and bows to the idol before getting up and moving to the living room area. The lights come up on that area as she picks up a notebook from a shelf or table and goes to the door. She appears to be doing all this on 'automatic'.

She opens the door and as a matter of routine opens the book. She looks up and is disconcerted to find a stranger before her.

DEEPAK. Namaste, Auntie ji.

Shanta stares at him, not sure what to say or do.

DEEPAK. My name is Deepak. I spoke to you on the phone the other day.

SHANTA. Deepak?

DEEPAK. Mala's friend.

SHANTA. Mala is not at home.

DEEPAK. I know. I have come to meet you.

SHANTA. To meet me?

DEEPAK. If you recall, I spoke with you on the phone, about meeting you.

SHANTA. Oh!

DEEPAK *(repeating it now as if to someone who doesn't understand)*. I called to ask if I could come and see you.

SHANTA. Mala will be returning at 7 o'clock. Please come then.

DEEPAK. But I came to meet you.

SHANTA *(pleading)*. Please come later.

DEEPAK. You are expecting someone else?

SHANTA. I–I thought you were the paper-wallah.

DEEPAK *(patiently)*. Auntie ji, you said I could come and meet you. It is very important that I talk to you.

SHANTA. Why? Please go away before Mala comes.

DEEPAK. Why?

SHANTA. She was very angry when I said you were coming.

DEEPAK. I told you not to let her know. That was the whole point!

SHANTA. Please, I beg of you! If she finds out you are here and I talked to you . . .

DEEPAK. What will she do? She can't kill you!

SHANTA. You don't know her.

The man walks into the house and heads straight to the kitchen, much to the surprise of Deepak.

The man, as the paper-wallah, wears a synthetic shirt and khaki trousers, with worn-out chappals.

Shanta goes back to 'automatic' and steps back in, opening the book and looking at the accounts.

Deepak uses this opportunity to come right in.

MAN *(entering from kitchen).* No gas smell now. I told you it was the tube.

DEEPAK. I thought he is the paper-wallah.

MAN. That is right. I also help Madam with small things. There is no man in the house, that is why. If there is a man in the house, what is my problem whether her gas is leaking or her terrace is leaking. *(Turning to Shanta and speaking with the authority of a man.)* Hahn. Have you kept the money ready? Quickly.

Shanta has been looking down while the paper-wallah made his comment on her situation. The man easily towers over her, pelvis thrust out in an imposing manner, making Shanta very uneasy.

SHANTA *(reading from the book).* Six hundred and twenty rupees.

She offers the money to him which is between the pages of the book.

MAN *(giving her a bill).* No. It is six hundred and eighty.

SHANTA. But I have written it down! Every day's account!

MAN *(snatching the book from her).* Show.

The man shakes his head while reading. He returns the book back to her.

MAN. Some entry must have been forgotten. Here is the bill.

SHANTA. But I write it as soon as I get the magazine or paper.

MAN *(very sure of himself, not at all threatening).* You are wrong. It is six hundred and ninety. Look at the bill.

SHANTA. But I never forget to write it in the book!

MAN. I will come back later and take it from your daughter.

Pause.

SHANTA. No. No. Why trouble her? *(Rising.)* I will give you the balance money.

Shanta gives him the money in his hand and exits to get the rest.

Deepak sits down on the sofa.

The two men stare at each other.

DEEPAK. They must take a lot of magazines from you.

MAN *(without blinking)*. Femina. Elle. Cosmopolitan. All ...

Shanta enters and gives the man some more money.

The man exits.

DEEPAK. You shouldn't allow people to walk right into your house. *(Laughing.)* Look at me. I just walked right into your house. At least you know the paper-wallah. *(More serious.)* Let me not waste your time. I am here to talk to you about Mala. But first let me tell you something about myself. I am Deepak Bhatia ... I am Colonel Bhatia's son.

Shanta looks at him now in a new light.

SHANTA. Deepak? Why did you not tell me you are Colonel Bhatia's son? I have seen you when you were so small!

DEEPAK. My father conveys his regards to you.

SHANTA. Why didn't you tell me on the phone?

DEEPAK. Didn't Mala tell you? *(Looking at Shanta's uneasiness.)* Looks like she hasn't told you a lot of things.

Pause.

Shanta gets up.

SHANTA. Just one minute.

Shanta goes to the phone and begins to dial.

DEEPAK. Are you calling Mala?

Shanta does not respond.

Deepak goes to her.

DEEPAK. She is not in her office. And she has switched off her cellphone.

Deepak takes the phone from her hand and puts it down.

DEEPAK. Please. Can I talk to you, Auntie? For Mala's sake!

Shanta looks at him, not knowing what to do.

DEEPAK *(gently)*. Please.

SHANTA. She will be very angry with me. You must go now! What if she comes home and . . . please!

Deepak looks at her for a while, then takes charge by putting on the posture of the man, pelvis thrust forward, taking charge of the space.

DEEPAK. No. I will not leave. But I will make a deal with you . . . I won't tell Mala that you let me in. So—if you don't tell her we had a talk, she won't know. So she won't be angry with you.

Shanta looks at him, thinking about it.

DEEPAK. I promise I won't tell her. Scout's honour.

SHANTA. She may come home right now.

DEEPAK. Has she ever been home at this time of the day?

SHANTA *(after a while, a bit more sure)*. Sit down.

Deepak sits down on the sofa.

Shanta sits at a little distance from him.

DEEPAK. Have you any idea at all where she is right now?

SHANTA. At the office.

DEEPAK. No, she isn't, and you know it . . . *(Leaning forward.)* Look, didn't she say anything at all about me?

SHANTA. Yes . . . She does not want to see you.

DEEPAK. Before that. Did she tell you that we were . . . seeing each other?

SHANTA *(shaking her head)*. No.

DEEPAK *(really hurt by this)*. Oh.

SHANTA. When I told her you had called, she said she doesn't want to see you again . . . she told me not to let you inside the house.

DEEPAK. I just don't get it. I thought everything was going well. *(Upset.)* I thought she loved me. Maybe I said or did something to upset her. But what could it be? . . . *(Composing himself.)* Last week, I told her that she was the most intelligent, sensitive and dynamic woman I had met. She just stared at me and said, 'I have something to tell you. It is over. I don't want to continue with our relationship.' She doesn't want to see me ever again.

SHANTA. She said that?

DEEPAK. Yes.

SHANTA. There was nothing else you said?

DEEPAK. Like?

SHANTA. That you did not want to marry her?

DEEPAK *(shocked)*. No! On the contrary! . . . Did she say I did not want to marry her?

SHANTA. Yes.

DEEPAK. I thought she never told you anything about me.

SHANTA. She didn't say it like that. I thought—I thought that, something she said made me feel . . . that you did not want to marry her.

DEEPAK. But that's not true! . . . What did she say to make you feel that way?

SHANTA. After she said she never wanted to see you again—she said—'That is the way it is with men.' That is why I thought that you . . .

DEEPAK. That just doesn't make sense. I have never ever given her the feeling that I am only interested in a casual affair. In fact, I went out of my way to show how much I respect her as a person.

SHANTA *(gently, with hope)*. Do you want to marry my daughter?

Deepak nods.

SHANTA. And your parents?

DEEPAK. Our fathers were friends. My parents would be happy to know that . . . *(Knowing this would get her on his side.)* But it doesn't look like it's going to happen. I guess that's the end of that.

SHANTA *(hastily)*. No, don't say that! She is a very nice girl at heart. Sometimes she gets angry with me but . . . It is always my fault . . . I—I forget things. I am the one to blame. But she is a very nice girl at heart. If she settles down, she will be all right.

DEEPAK. What do you mean by 'all right'? Do you feel there is something wrong?

SHANTA. No, no. What am I saying? I mean that everything will be all right.

DEEPAK. There is something you are not telling me.

SHANTA. It is my fault only. I will feel easy once she settles down.

DEEPAK. Auntie ji, I want to continue to meet your daughter. You must help me.

SHANTA. I also want you to meet her and—and take her to meet your parents.

DEEPAK. But you know she won't. She has been avoiding my calls ever since we last met. Only you can help now.

SHANTA. Tell me what you want me to do and I will do it. How can I help?

DEEPAK. I don't know. By telling me what is worrying you about your daughter. There is something that you are not telling me.

Pause.

DEEPAK. Trust me.

SHANTA. Promise me you won't tell her anything.

DEEPAK. You have nothing to fear.

Pause.

SHANTA. She tells me she is going someplace, and she ... Oh, why should I, her own mother, say all this to you? You will not like her then.

DEEPAK. I am here to help Mala, believe me.

SHANTA. About a month ago, she told me she was going on Holi for a picnic to Palam Vihar with her office friends. But the next day, I overheard her talking on the phone to her office friend, saying that she had to spend Holi with me. Why? Why should she tell lies? To her friend and to me? As if I could stop her from going anywhere ... She keeps on telling me lies. Sometimes she repeats the same lies, as if she does not care if I know she is lying ... But please don't think bad of her. There are times when she is at home early from work and spends the whole evening reading magazines. She feels very restless then. That is when we quarrel. She is fine when she has work, or when she goes out. That is why I feel sometimes, thank God she is going out. At least then she looks—happy. But I am her mother. I must worry about her. I pray for her. I never pray for myself. Only for her happiness.

Pause.

DEEPAK. I know where she was on Holi.

SHANTA. She told you?

DEEPAK. She was with me.

SHANTA. With you? Oh! I always think the worst. But why so much hiding?

DEEPAK. We met at a friend's party a couple of days earlier. She smiled at me and wanted to dance with me. We got talking about her work. I dropped her here that night and we arranged to spend Holi together as we were both free. We were seeing each other every day after that. Very soon I wanted to meet you right away. But somehow, she didn't want it. She has other plans. God alone knows what they are. Last Monday she told me in no uncertain terms that she . . . *(Shrugs his shoulders.)* I just don't understand it. What did I do wrong?

SHANTA *(thinking about something else).* Monday?

Shanta opens the book once again.

SHANTA. She bought some magazines that evening. She was very depressed. She . . . There is something else.

Shanta gets up.

SHANTA. One minute. I will get it for you.

Shanta exits to another room.

Pause.

The phone rings. Deepak answers the phone.

DEEPAK. Hello?

A long pause as there is no response.

Shanta enters with a calendar. She looks at Deepak on the phone.

SHANTA. Who is it?

Shanta hands him the calendar and takes the phone.

Deepak looks at the calendar.

SHANTA *(on the phone).* Hello?

DEEPAK *(looking at the calendar).* There's a cross on last Monday's date!

SHANTA *(terrified, her pitch rising).* Mala! . . . No. No! I tried to but he just came in! Mala! Please! I will tell him to go away! I will tell him to go away right now! . . . No. Don't say that! Come home! Mala, please come home!

Deepak stares at the calendar. He flips the pages backwards and looks at the previous months.

Shanta sobs as she puts down the phone.

The music builds up.

SHANTA. Please go away. Please go away!

Blackout.

Mala's voice on tape as before.

MALA. I don't know why. I just don't understand . . . Please don't ask me why I do it. It's just a game . . . not a game. No . . . it's . . . I know it's wrong. What I am doing is terribly wrong! But it means a lot to me. I like it. That is why I am a bad person. I have no character . . . I suppose it's these Western values. I wish I were more traditional, then I wouldn't behave like this . . . No, no, that's stupid. I know that's very easy, to put the blame elsewhere . . . *(Listening to the counsellor.)* It has to end in a month's time. In fact I like it best when I can time it so it lasts for thirty days. I even mark it on my calendar. After that, I have to—move on, if you know what I mean . . . Well, it means that it is no longer satisfying to me, and I don't mean the physical part of it, although that is usually the main attraction for me . . . Not that I actually enjoy it when they are doing it to me . . . Sometimes I do, with the right kind of people . . . The right kind of people are, let me see . . . usually older men, though not necessarily so; Deepak, my fiancé, is only a few years older to me . . . I think I like it—I don't know how to put it . . . When they—sort of— you know—use me . . . *(Listening to the counsellor.)* I don't know. I can't explain it. The only person who can, who could have prevented all this is my mother. Sometimes I wish she would just tell me to stop. She could have prevented a lot from happening . . . Here are all the names of people whom I have been with. And the outline . . . well, I just wanted a line that would put them all altogether. But if you ask me, whose face I think it is—it must be my mother's.

> *Lights come on a party in progress. Music. The man is seen talking to someone on his right. In the far corner, Mala is on her cellphone. She is dressed provocatively but not in a manner that is flashy or revealing. Although the room is full of people, we only see Mala and the man.*
>
> *Night.*

MALA. Hmm. I am not so sure whether it works.

Mala is talking to someone, presumably a colleague. She has her back to the Man who is talking with someone else.

MALA. To start with, I don't think she should be skipping rope with her daughter. That's not real freedom. It is still very gender constructed ... If you ask me she should be playing cricket with her daughter and husband. You have to say it all in fifteen seconds. The important point is her physical ease and freedom. Start with her batting. A perfect hit. She makes two runs with her daughter. Then show her bowling while her husband is batting. He makes a snide remark about her being irritable because it is that time of the month. She bowls, hits him straight in the crotch. He runs yelping into the house. She tosses the ball in the air. Freeze. Caption. A hit always. Perfectly in control, all through the month. Cloud 9—sanitary napkins. That's enough ... Oh, sure we could work on it together. I will come in early tomorrow. Okay? And one more thing—go easy on the cigarettes. *(Digging out her cellphone.)* Excuse me, I have to make a call.

Mala walks to a corner while she waits for someone to answer it. She stops, stunned for a while to hear Deepak's voice first and then her mother's.

MALA *(on the phone).* How could you let him in the house? What did I tell you? Why can't you just do what I tell you to do? I am not coming home! If I go away somewhere it will be your fault!

Mala puts her cellphone in her bag, takes a deep breath, and clears her mind of the conversation with her mother. She looks around and notices the man. Mala walks up to the man and stands next to him. The man as Ravi is wearing a business suit. He wears gold-rimmed glasses. He notices her standing there. Their eyes meet. She looks directly at him with her eyes wide open almost in fear. She can't help but give the impression she is interested in the man.

MAN. Hi. Haven't we met before?

MALA *(not at all as articulate as before)*. I—I am Mala.

MAN *(smiling)*. The Bronze Beauty Campaign, right?

MALA. Right.

MAN. You deserved the IAAFA award. One of the best campaigns I have come across in my years in advertising. You are a genius.

MALA *(almost as if he has offended her)*. Shall we talk about something else apart from work? *(At once apologetic.)* I am sorry, I didn't mean . . .

MAN. Oh don't be. We are at a party, so why talk shop . . . *(Changing the subject.)* Oh this is my fiancée, Radhika. *(To Radhika.)* This is Mala. One of our most . . . *(Checking himself.)* She is with our Delhi creative department.

MALA. Hello . . . Oh! This is my favourite tune.

Mala looks straight at the man. Her eyes telling him to dance with her.

MAN. Would you—like to dance?

MALA. I am not so sure, whether . . . if it is okay with you, Radhika. *(Rising.)* Thanks . . . Would you mind my bag for me please? . . . Thanks.

Ravi leads Mala on to the dance floor. They move to the centre of the space. Ravi holds her, casting a quick glance in Radhika's direction. They dance.

MAN. You dance very well.

MALA. No, I don't. You are saying that just to please me.

MAN. No. Not at all—I—Oh yeah, sure. I could teach you the salsa some time . . . So I hear a lot of things about you.

MALA. Oh.

MAN. From the office. Rahul was telling me . . . You have been with him for some time I think.

MALA *(sighing)*. So how long are you going to be in town?

MAN. For about a month I guess.

MALA. Perfect.

MAN. Huh?

MALA. How long have you known Radhika?

MAN. For about five years. We will be marr ed in a few months. But—I would like to get to know you better.

MALA. Hold me closer.

The man moves closer to her, his arm slippin ; from her back closer to her waist.

MAN. Yes ... You have a nice body.

MALA. Thank you.

They look at each other.

MALA. Hold me closer.

They dance for a while, with the man explorin g her back more with his hand when it is away from Ra hika's line of vision.

MAN. Look, why don't I take Radhika home anc you could— you know—come over to my hotel tomorrow? For a drink. Hmm?

MALA. Take me to your room with you now.

MAN. No. No ... I—I can't. I am with her ton ;ht.

MALA *(pleading, looking up at him to be kissed)*. Do whatever you want with me, but take me with you now.

MAN. No, don't get too close. Later, okay? Oh ny God! She is coming here.

The man breaks away abruptly as Radhika presumably pulls them apart.

MAN. Radhika, no! I was just being polite and dan :ing with her.

Mala stands to one side, humiliated.

MAN. I am sorry, I ... Look, don't be angry witr me. She was leading me on. I swear it was her fault. Wha could I do? Radhika!

The man follows Radhika in a hurry without even a glance at Mala. Mala follows, head held down like a schoolgirl caught in the act. She looks around at all the people who are staring at her. Mala fights her tears. She covers her face, picks up her bag and leaves.

Fade to the living room.

Later.

Mala walks from the party area into the living room area. The music fades out. Mala unlocks the door and lets herself in. She drops her bag on the sofa and stands there for a while, not knowing what to do. She sits on the sofa and stares into space. The lights come on and Shanta enters.

MALA. What do you want?

SHANTA. Have you eaten? Shall I make some roti for you?

MALA. No. I am not hungry.

SHANTA *(whining)*. Eat something, no.

MALA *(sharp)*. Go to sleep! Go!

Shanta begins to leave, switching off some lights.

MALA. What did he say to you?

SHANTA. The man wanted extra money, I gave him.

MALA. I mean the man you let inside my house. The man I told you not to let inside the house! What did he say to you about me?

SHANTA. I don't remember. Please, I have a headache.

MALA. You forget! As usual. You forget what you don't want to deal with!

SHANTA. Please, Mala, I am not feeling well.

MALA. I don't care if you are not feeling well, Mummy. Because I don't know whether you are telling the truth or simply trying to escape as always. What did he tell you?

Shanta turns to the portrait of Shri Krishna and does not respond to Mala's question.

MALA. Stop looking at that picture!

SHANTA *(still looking at the picture)*. He told me he wanted to marry you.

MALA. Always staring at that picture whenever you want to avoid something.

SHANTA. That boy wants to marry you.

MALA. One of these days I will throw that picture out of the house.

SHANTA *(looking at her, mildly)*. But you are the one avoiding the subject now.

MALA *(staring at her)*. I don't want to marry him.

SHANTA. No. You will have to. This is like my prayers have been answered. All these years I have been waiting for this. I have always listened to you for everything, but this. You must say yes.

MALA. I won't.

SHANTA. Why? He is such a nice boy and from a family we know. What more do you want? What more can anyone ask for?

MALA. I have my reasons.

SHANTA. What reasons?

MALA. I won't tell you . . . I don't have to tell you anything. Go to bed.

SHANTA. You can tell me what is troubling you. I am always there for you.

MALA. That's not true. You are never there . . . You never have been.

SHANTA. What have I done to deserve this?

MALA. You don't want me to tell you that, do you?

SHANTA. Please tell me where I have gone wrong so I can say sorry to you.

MALA. You forget. You forget so easily.

SHANTA. No. That is not true! Why are you punishing me like this?

MALA. It is true. It did happen, but you never believed me.

SHANTA *(turning away)*. I don't know what you are talking about. I will prepare alu parantha for you tomorrow, you always like that for breakfast.

MALA. That is how you always pacified me and that is how I know that you believe me, deep down. Oh yes, you would remember that I always like alu paranthas because that's what I got whenever I came to you, hurt and crying. Instead of listening to what I had to say, you stuffed me with food. I couldn't speak because I was being fed all the time, and you know what? I began to like them. I thought that was the cure for my pain. That if I ate till I was stuffed, the pain would go away. Every time I came to you, Mummy, you were ready with something to feed me. You knew. Otherwise you wouldn't have been so prepared. You knew all along what was happening to me, and I won't ever let you forget that!

SHANTA *(turning to the portrait)*. I put myself at the feet of my God. He knows what I am going through. Only my Krishna knows . . .

MALA. That is the trouble! *(Going to her.)* That has always been the trouble! You were never there for me. You were too busy *(Pointing to the portrait, saying the word with contempt.)* praying!

Shanta closes her eyes and begins to pray.

MALA. For what? And for whom? Surely not for me! . . . *(Yelling.)* Stop praying! . . . I said stop that! *(Turning Shanta around.)* Look at me!

SHANTA. Go away! Go away or tell me what you want from me!

MALA. It's no use now. You should have said that twenty years ago!

SHANTA. Why this punishment? Why this punishment, because you fell down the stairs and broke your leg?

Mala stares at her.

SHANTA. It is my fault that I should have simply asked you where it hurt and kissed you, put you in my lap and rocked you to sleep singing a lori. Instead I gave you sweets and went to my pooja. That is my fault.

MALA. I cannot believe it. I simply cannot believe that . . . Do you really think that is what I am talking about? Ask yourself honestly. Tell me if you honestly believe that is what I am talking about. Tell me. No, don't look at your God, look at me, look me in the eye and tell me—'Yes, that is all that you are talking about.'

SHANTA *(looking at her with wide-eyed innocence)*. What else are you talking about?

MALA. Ma, I am talking about what I had told you five years ago, but you said it wasn't true, it couldn't be true. But now I know that you want to believe it is not true.

SHANTA. Five years ago? You didn't tell me anything . . .

MALA. Five years ago, six years ago, I can't remember exactly when! We were in the kitchen and we were talking about that rape case that was in the papers. You said something about children also not being safe. Don't you remember anything at all? Then I told you about—what happened to me. But you changed the subject. At that time I wondered . . . Is it just me? Did I imagine it all? Surely not. No. It did happen.

SHANTA. Mala, I don't remember. Please forgive me. Maybe I said something in my foolish way and you took it seriously.

MALA. No. No, Ma. I think it was the other way round. I said something serious and you took it lightly. Yes, yes I am sure you did that deliberately.

SHANTA. No, no, Mala. Just forget all these bad dreams and . . .

MALA. I am not talking about a bad dream! I am talking about the time when Uncle Vinay would molest me. When I was seven. Then eight. Nine. Ten. Every vacation when we went to visit him or when he came to stay with us. You were busy in either the pooja room or the kitchen. I would go to Papa and cry. Before I could even tell him why I was crying, he would tell me to go to you. You always fed me and—and you never said it but I knew what you were saying to me without words. That I should eat well and go to sleep and the pain will go away. And, and—Oh God! It did go away. But it comes back. It didn't go away for ever!

SHANTA *(really puzzled)*. Mala, my daughter. What all have you been thinking all these years? You have always been so bold and frank. But sometimes, you tell stories.

MALA. This is not a story I made up and you know it.

SHANTA. If it were true I would have said something. Now go to sleep and we will talk about this boy Deepak tomorrow. Such a good family he is from . . .

MALA *(screaming)*. Listen to me!

Shanta covers her ears more for the scream than not wanting to listen to her.

MALA. No. No . . . It is so easy for you, because you can hide behind *(Pointing to the picture.)* this! Just forget what you don't want to know and then pray. I won't let you get off so easily. There is only one way I can make you listen to me. By taking this away from you!

Mala takes down the portrait. Shanta tries to prevent her.

SHANTA. Mala, what are you doing? Please don't! No, no, don't—

MALA. I can't let you hide behind this all the time!

SHANTA *(hanging on to the portrait)*. I will do anything you say, but leave my Krishna alone!

MALA. Let me go—!

SHANTA. Please, no!

Mala finally manages to break free and takes the painting to the main door.

SHANTA *(aghast)*. What are you doing? NO!

Mala flings the painting out of the door. We hear a crash and the breaking of glass. Shanta rushes out. Mala is slowly regaining her composure. She sits down on the sofa. Shanta re-enters with the portrait and the pieces of glass on the portrait. She begins to cry.

MALA. I am sorry, Ma. If I had done that a long time ago ... Then maybe ...

SHANTA. You don't know what you have done. You don't know what you have done!

Shanta places the portrait on a table and turns to look at Mala.

SHANTA *(going to Mala)*. Yes. Yes, I remember now.

MALA. It's okay. We don't have to talk about it if you don't want to.

SHANTA. No, no. I want to talk. I remember, but what I remember is not what you remember. I had forgotten it, but now ...

MALA. It doesn't matter now. I just have to learn to live with the pain.

SHANTA. Not just the pain. I remember, much as I was trying to forget, what I saw. Not when you were seven but when you were thirteen. *(Gently.)* Please don't misunderstand me, Mala. I remember, seeing you with my brother during the summer holidays. You were pushing yourself on him in the bedroom.

MALA. No! That's not true!

SHANTA. I remember, Mala. You want me to remember? You were telling him to kiss you.

MALA. No.

SHANTA. To touch you.

MALA. I didn't—

SHANTA. To pinch your—breasts.

MALA. Stop it!

SHANTA. You were forcing him to say things to you.

MALA. Stop it, I said!

SHANTA. To do things to you.

MALA. I did not! I did not!

SHANTA. That is why I forget. I went to the kitchen to vomit. Then I prayed. I prayed for you Mala. *(Pointing to the portrait.)* That is what I was praying to. To our God, so He could send his Sudarshan Chakra to defend you, to defend us from the demon inside you, not outside you. But you wouldn't let me. You don't let me.

MALA *(crying)*. No!

SHANTA. I remember other things also. When your cousin, your father's nephew came for his holidays.

MALA. He made the advances. He found out from Uncle ...

SHANTA. No, Mala!

MALA. Why don't you believe me? He told me that I was Uncle's reference! Those were his words! 'Your Uncle Vinay has given me your reference!' Uncle told him, Ma! I didn't do or say anything to him. He came to my room! Once he said Uncle's name, I just couldn't stop him!

SHANTA. Why should you stop him? You were enjoying it. Your cousin told me in private that he was concerned about you, that I should not send you out of the house.

MALA. That was after! He told you that after he molested me!

SHANTA. But Mala, I have seen it with my own eyes. You enjoyed it. You were an average child but you had my brother and your cousins dancing around you. That is what you wanted. Yes! How can I forget? I am trying to forget, please help me forget.

Silence.

MALA *(quietly)*. Yes. You are right.

SHANTA. And please don't talk about trying to forget the pain ... Try to forget the pleasure.

MALA. That is part of the pain, Ma. The pleasure is part of the pain. *(Composing herself.)* I—I will try, Ma. I can only try.

SHANTA. I forget. I forget everything. Be like me

MALA. Yes.

SHANTA. You have been a very bad girl, you have gone astray. But Krishna will show you the way.

MALA. Yes, Ma.

SHANTA. And please meet that boy Deepak. I will invite his father next week to come and see you.

Mala looks at her helplessly.

SHANTA. That is the only way. Krishna has sent him for you.

Mala nods. Mala gets up.

SHANTA. And Mala ... Don't say anything about all this to him. You understand? If I had known what those marks on your calendar meant, I would not have shown it to him. You are lucky he is so understanding. But this ... Nobody will forgive this. God help us if his father comes to know ... This is your only chance.

MALA. How can I hide all this from him if I am to marry him, Ma?

SHANTA. If you forget it ever happened, then you won't have anything to hide.

The two women look at each other. Mala straightens up.

MALA *(speaking sharply as before)*. Go to sleep. I don't want you complaining that I keep you up all night.

SHANTA *(subservient as before, switching off the lights).* Yes, Mala.

MALA *(exiting).* Where are the magazines that I had ordered?

SHANTA *(exiting).* In your room, Mala ...

Fade to:

Music. A restaurant. Mala walks slowly from the living room area on to the special area, which is now a restaurant. Deepak is seated. He rises when he sees her. They sit down. The music fades out.

DEEPAK. Thank you for seeing me.

MALA *(formal).* You are welcome.

DEEPAK. What will you have?

MALA. Just a coffee, please.

DEEPAK *(signalling to a waiter).* One more coffee over here, please. *(Sipping his coffee, which is mimed.)* Are you okay?

MALA. Yes. I think.

DEEPAK. So what's with the thirty-day affairs?

MALA. I am not sure you will understand.

DEEPAK. I want to understand. Make me understand.

The Man walks in and sits at a table. Deepak ignores him. He is wearing a T-shirt and jeans, and a cap.

MALA. You know I have been ... around.

DEEPAK. I gathered from your calendar. That was some collection of ticks, crosses and names.

MALA. Why do you like me? Why?

DEEPAK. You are talented, beautiful, intelligent, honest. You have a rare gift of honesty. I have yet to meet a person as honest as you. Mala, I am a very patient man. I am willing to do what it takes to win your trust and to get to know the real person in you.

MALA *(unmoved).* I don't know. I should feel something, right? I should be thrilled. But I am not. It doesn't mean a thing to me.

DEEPAK. Then what do you want? What is it that you want the most?

The waiter presumably serves her coffee. Mala looks up. At the same time the Man catches the waiter's eye and gestures for the waiter to go to him.

MALA. Did you see that?

DEEPAK. What?

MALA. The man over there.

DEEPAK. What about him?

MALA. He was staring at my breasts.

Deepak is angry. He gets up and goes to the Man.

MALA *(startled)*. Deepak, no!

DEEPAK *(to Man)*. Excuse me.

MAN *(looking up)*. Huh?

Mala goes to Deepak and holds him by the arm.

DEEPAK. Were you staring at my girlfriend?

MAN *(horrified at the thought)*. No! That's not true!

MALA *(pulling him)*. Deepak, let's go.

MAN. How dare you insult me like that?

DEEPAK. She said you were staring at her and that's good enough for me to know that you were.

MAN. Well, she is mistaken or she is lying.

Deepak raises his fist. The Man rises.

MALA *(shouting)*. I made that up!

Deepak looks at her.

MALA *(taking Deepak back to their table)*. I made it up. Sit down.

The Man walks out of the restaurant in a huff. Deepak sits down, taken aback.

DEEPAK. Did you say that just to avoid trouble?

Mahesh Dattani

MALA. No. He wasn't staring at me ... I wanted him to ... You want to know what I feel the most? ... If he had looked at me, I would have felt—I would have felt—truly alive.

Pause.

Deepak throws his hands up in despair.

DEEPAK. This is just too ... This can't go on. It just can't go on.

MALA. I told you so. I know it won't work between us.

DEEPAK. No. It won't work between us because you are not even trying. Can't you at least try? Do something about it?

MALA. What do you want me to do? I am being honest with you about what I feel, but what can I do?

DEEPAK. I don't know. See a psychiatrist or somebody.

MALA. I am not mentally ill or anything ...

DEEPAK. But you do need help.

MALA *(sighing)*. Maybe. Maybe, you are right.

Freeze. Slow fade-out while the tape plays the same conversation as the first. Except this time, the sound is processed almost to a point of distortion. Some of the key words reverberate so they overlap over each other.

MALA'S VOICE. Today is the 30th of September ... 2001, and my name is *(Reverberate 'name is'.)* ... I don't think I want to say my name ... I am sorry. *(Reverberate 'sorry'.)* I hope that is okay with you ... I am unsure about this ... and a lot of other things. But this ... This is the first time you see that I ... *(Reverberate 'first time'.)* I know it is all my fault, really ... *(Reverberate 'my fault' almost till the end of the tape.)* It must be. I must have asked for it ... Somehow, I just seem to be made for it. Maybe I was born that way, maybe ... This is what I am meant for. It's not anybody's fault, except my own. Sometimes I wish that my mother ... I am sorry but ...

Spot on Shanta in the prayer room.

Music.

MALA'S VOICE. I can only tell you more if you turn this thing off.

The tape continues to hiss for a while. The lights brighten on Shanta as the music builds up. Quick blackout.

End of Act One.

ACT II

The counsellor's office as in the first scene. Mala is seated in exactly the same spot in the same clothes as in Scene One. In fact it is a continuation of that session. However, this conversation is interspersed with Mala's voice on tape four years ago. The doll is not visible in this scene, and there is no blackout during Mala's voice on tape except at the end. The focus stays on the confident new Mala even when the tape is playing.

MALA *(self-assured and easy)*. I feel I want to tell it to people who would understand. It's like starting all over again. It's like you never had those scars.

MALA'S VOICE ON TAPE ... My father left us, for another woman ... I feel if I were more lovable he would have at least visited us ... We continue to get money from him every month, and he pays the rent ... but I haven't seen him in fifteen years ... I ... don't think my mother and he got along—that way. Again, because of me ...

MALA. It's like taking off the bandages on your face after a bloody car crash that left your face all scarred beyond recognition, as if you didn't have a face at all. To wake up after many many years, as if from a coma ... And to let the bandages come off ... and suddenly discover a whole new face again. All of a sudden you feel that you are—entitled to life.

MALA'S VOICE ON TAPE. I have been so bad, I can't tell you where to begin! It's not just the men in the office I told you about, but before ... much before! I—Oh God! I—I seduced my uncle when I was thirteen! I—slept with my cousin—and—anyone who was available ... No, there is nothing to tell about my uncle, forget all that, please help me stop this behaviour.

MALA. I can smile again. I can be a little girl, again. Not again, but for the first time. At thirty-plus, I am the little girl I never was. I want to see movies, taste ice cream. Really taste it, feel the high from the sugar. Tell the difference between flavours. I hear sounds I never cared to hear before—birds, temple bells ... My senses are working again. I can touch this chair and feel the chair touch me. My whole body can feel! And for the first time I enjoyed sex. Truly enjoyed it for its tactile pleasure. Not as a craving for some kind of approval. I came alive and experienced what it means to be really loved. And for once I could look at Deepak in the eyes and say 'I love you' to him and believe it when he says the same to me.

Fade to black. Mala's voice on tape as before. The light comes up on the doll once again.

MALA'S VOICE *(she cries)*. My uncle just went away. He left me. He said he was disgusted with me—my behaviour. He never returned ... But now he is coming back. He is coming home ... Please understand he is not a bad person or anything like that ... I am so confused, I don't know what I feel for him ... I know you are not supposed to tell me what I am to do, I am to figure that out for myself, right?

Fade in:

The living room. Shanta brings in two cups of tea. Mala is flipping through a magazine. Shanta places Mala's cup of tea in front of her. Shanta sits at the far end of the sofa with her tea, sipping it nervously. The nervousness spreads to Mala. She too sips her tea nervously.

SHANTA *(after a while)*. He will be here for two days.

MALA. Maybe I should leave now.

SHANTA. If it is getting late for you ...

MALA. No. It's okay. I can wait for a while.

SHANTA. There is no need. You can meet him in the evening.

MALA. You said he is coming to Delhi on work.

SHANTA. Yes.

MALA. Can't his company put him up in a hotel?

SHANTA. Mala . . . You said it was all right for him to stay with us. So—I told him to stay here.

MALA. Oh. Yes, yes. It is perfectly all right. There's no need to—avoid anybody.

SHANTA. Yes. After all, he has helped us so much after your father left us.

MALA. In what way has he helped us?

SHANTA. If you have finished with those magazines, I can give them to the ruddi-wallah today.

MALA. I hate it when you avoid answering questions! In what way has he helped us?

SHANTA. I don't know . . .

MALA. Tell me!

SHANTA *(looking away, more nervous than before).* Mala, I am sorry; I should have told you but . . . The money that we kept receiving after your father left us was from your uncle.

MALA. And Father? Didn't he send us anything at all?

SHANTA. Nothing.

MALA. No communication from him?

Shanta shakes her head.

MALA. But you pretended it came from him. You lied. *(Imitating her.)* Oh look! Daddy has sent us some extra money for Diwali. He wanted to come to your school day celebration but he has sent you some money for a new dress for you! *(Shrugging it off.)* Oh what does it matter? It doesn't make a difference to me. *(Getting up.)* I don't think I am going to wait for him.

Mala walks to pick up her bag.

SHANTA. I lied for you. So that you will feel that your father was thinking about you.

MALA *(stopping)*. Oh no. Oh I won't let you get away with that. You know why he left us. So don't try to pretend you tried very hard to show me that he loved me, but at the same time giving me the impression that actually he didn't. He left you, not me. I know he didn't care about me, but he didn't leave because of me. He left because of you. You didn't love him. The only reason you shared my room was because you didn't want to sleep with him. All night long I had to listen to your mumbling, saying you didn't want him near you. You didn't want him touching you. You even moved that horrible picture of your god into my room saying he will protect us . . . I remember Daddy's last words to me. You know what he said. He said to me, 'I married a frozen woman.' A frozen woman. So don't try to tell me that you were concerned about me by hiding the truth. The only truth you want to hide is your failure as a wife and a mother.

Shanta gets up slowly and begins to leave.

MALA. Am I right?

SHANTA. I have to wash the clothes and change the sheets.

MALA. I am right.

SHANTA *(turning around)*. Yes. You are right. I may not be a good wife or mother. But at least I am a good servant.

Shanta picks up the tea cups.

SHANTA. I have my God and that is enough for me. Krishna knows what all I have gone through. He knows.

The Man enters, as Vinay. He is dressed in a business shirt and tie, with his coat slung casually over his shoulders or over his arm. He carries an overnight bag. He notices Shanta and ignores Mala.

MAN. Hello, Shanta! How are you?

He goes to Shanta and pats her on the arm.

MALA *(under her breath).* Uncle!

The Man turns around to her.

MAN. Hello, Mala. Off somewhere. *(Turning back to Shanta.)* So how have you been, my dear sister?

Mala walks towards him slowly.

MALA. No. I—I . . .

Mala turns around quickly and exits through the main door. Shanta looks in the direction of Mala. Music. Blackout.

ACT III

The living room. The Man enters with a shirt in his hand.

MAN. Shanta!

Shanta enters from the kitchen.

SHANTA. Yes? Dinner will be ready in half an hour.

MAN *(tossing the shirt at her).* I was just wondering whether you could iron this shirt for me. You know how have always been hopeless at these things.

SHANTA. I will do it tonight.

MAN. I hate to trouble you two like this.

SHANTA. No trouble, Bhaiya.

MAN. That is the only reason why I stay in a hotel when I am in Delhi.

SHANTA. You sit and read or watch TV. I will take care of it afterwards.

MAN. But why did you ask me to stay with you?

SHANTA. I told you. About Deepak.

MAN. Yes. Finally! I was getting worried about that girl.

SHANTA. Sit down, Vinay bhaiya.

The Man sits down. Shanta joins him.

MAN *(innocent).* What is it?

SHANTA. Nothing. I just want to tell you that I want this to go through.

MAN. You mean, Deepak and Mala?

SHANTA. Yes. This is her only chance.

MAN. Yes, I understand.

SHANTA. So, I want you also to help. By meeting the boy and his parents. It will be of help. They knew her father very well you see and I don't want that coming in the way ...

MAN. Shanta, you know you can always rely on my help. That is nothing. Isn't she like my daughter also?

Shanta looks at him. The Man continues regardless.

MAN. Think nothing of it. I shall play the dutiful uncle tomorrow at dinner. In fact, I should interview the boy and see if he is suitable for our Mala. Isn't that right?

No response from Shanta. The Man waves his hand in front of her face.

MAN. You are off again. Ever since I can recall, you simply start dreaming whenever ... *(Making light of it.)* Remember when we were small, you would simply vanish into your own world ... like when we were having dinner and you nearly choked. If I didn't know the Heimlich manoeuvre from school, God alone knows ...

He looks at her. Shanta is staring at the spot where the painting was.

SHANTA *(as if it is a matter of grave concern).* I forgot to get the glass fixed.

The Man goes to where the picture is on the table. Lightning. Lights dim. Deepak's flat. Thunder can be heard at a distance. The lights come on to this side of the stage which is Deepak's living room. The lights also remain on the Man and Shanta. It is important the two scenes are played simultaneously without dimming or raising the lights. Mala's voice is heard, with the doorbell.

MALA *(offstage)*. Deepak!

Banging on a door. Deepak enters, slipping on a T-shirt. He is in pyjamas. He opens the door and lets her in.

DEEPAK. Are you all right?

MALA. I don't know. Can I stay with you?

DEEPAK. Of course. Come in. Can I make you some coffee?

Mala shakes her head sitting down. We see the Man examining the picture.

MALA. I–I don't know where to go!

The Man holds up the shards that are still on the picture.

MAN. How did this happen?

Deepak sits next to Mala.

MALA. Can I stay here?

SHANTA. What? Oh that. The picture just—fell down.

DEEPAK. Trust me Mala and tell me what is bothering you.

MAN. How can it just fall down? You must have pushed it while cleaning it.

MALA. Let's call it off, Deepak.

SHANTA. It's my fault. Yes.

DEEPAK. You are not giving yourself a chance. You are not giving me a chance.

MAN. You are too hard on yourself. It's nobody's fault.

DEEPAK. Help me connect with you!

Mala simply stares at him.

MAN. I will put these pieces aside for now. Be sure that the koodawali takes them away tomorrow.

Man begins to carefully pick the pieces off the picture and put them aside.

MALA. I am scared.

DEEPAK. Of what? Of whom?

MAN. I am glad you still have this picture. A memory of our mother.

MALA. I am scared to be home. I don't want to be home. Anywhere but home!

Lightning.

MAN. It's going to rain.

SHANTA. Yes.

Thunder.

DEEPAK. You can't go home anyway if it rains again. Why don't you stay here? I will fetch you a blanket. Hmm?

As Deepak gets up, Mala pulls him back.

MAN. There. Do you want me to put the picture back where it was?

SHANTA. Over there.

The Man puts the picture back on the wall.

MALA. There was a man following me.

MAN. There. No one can tell it's broken. But you better put the glass back soon.

MALA. I cannot stop them! I attract them.

DEEPAK. This is all in your mind.

MALA. You don't understand! I am doing something that attracts them to me.

MAN (*sitting down*). What is the matter? Is something wrong?

MALA. I want to. I want them to come to me.

DEEPAK. No. No, you don't.

MALA. It is true. If I were to let that man into my house, I will allow him to do anything.

DEEPAK. Mala, I met your counsellor yesterday.

MALA. What, what did she say?

DEEPAK. She didn't talk to me about you. She said that's confidential.

MALA. Then why did you go there?

DEEPAK. For myself. To find out how I can help you ... Are you upset because your uncle is visiting you?

MALA. No. No. What has he got to do with anything?

MAN. Why are you so silent?

SHANTA. Vinay Bhaiya, I am worried ...

MAN. About Mala? Don't worry. I will handle it all.

DEEPAK. I did mention this to the counsellor, just a hunch, you see ... She said nothing, but I could tell ...

SHANTA. She is—she—how can I say? How can I say anything?

MAN. I think I know what you are trying to say.

MALA *(avoiding talking about her uncle)*. No. It's not my uncle. It's my mother.

MAN. Is it me? Is it something to do with me?

   Shanta stares at him, clutching the cushion.

MALA. It's her. She doesn't want to see me happy.

DEEPAK. Why do you think that?

MAN. Tell me. Has it anything to do with me?

SHANTA. No!

MALA. She told you about my affairs, didn't she?

SHANTA. It's my fault. I should be more strict with Mala.

DEEPAK. I sort of got it out of her. Believe me she wasn't willing to talk.

SHANTA. It is so easy to slip into bad ways. I wish she would listen to me.

MALA. I wish she wouldn't be so lost in her religion. I wish she had been there for me!

DEEPAK. I am here for you now, and yet you make yourself inaccessible to me.

MAN. If there is any way I can help, just let me know.

SHANTA. Yes.

MALA. It's no use. I don't want you coming closer.

DEEPAK *(offering his hand)*. Hold my hand.

MALA. You don't understand. You just don't understand!

MAN. I am waiting. How may I help?

DEEPAK. Hold my hand. Forget everything and just touch me.

MALA. I—I can't. I don't want to. I can't!

SHANTA. Just make sure that the marriage happens. Just be there as if you were her father.

MAN. I have always been there like a father for her, in spite of everything.

Lightning. Spot on Shanta, lost in the photograph.

Mala slowly and very hesitantly reaches out to hold Deepak's hand. As she holds his hand . . .

Thunder.

The Man quickly enters their area. There is something very furtive in his eye movement and a sense of conspiracy in his tone of voice. It is not sexual but somehow urgent as if the job has to be done secretly and quickly. His gaze is fixed on Mala, except for his furtive glances. He exists only for Mala and not for Deepak.

DEEPAK. You see? It wasn't that difficult.

MAN. Touch me here.

Mala withdraws her hand sharply, frightened.

MAN. You don't love your uncle?

DEEPAK. What's wrong?

MAN. You don't love your uncle, hmm?

DEEPAK. Try it one more time.

MAN. Quickly, before someone sees you. Touch.

DEEPAK. Please, for my sake.

MAN. You said you loved me in front of Mummy and Daddy. Come on! Show it!

Mala hesitantly holds Deepak's hand.

DEEPAK. Thank you.

MAN. There! You feel that? It means I love you. Your uncle loves you.

Mala begins to cry.

DEEPAK *(stroking her hand gently).* It's okay. It's okay. Cry if you want to.

MAN. Shh! Don't cry. You want to come here during your holidays, no? Then don't cry. This is your seventh birthday, no? You are seven now. Ready for a real birthday present? Lie down. Come on, quickly.

DEEPAK. Look into my eyes.

MAN. If they hear you they will say you are a bad girl. This is our secret. *(Like an order but in a whisper.)* Don't cry!

Mala restrains herself from crying as if someone will hear her.

DEEPAK *(kneeling beside her).* Let go and trust me!

Mala begins to cry again, silently, looking at Deepak, terrified.

DEEPAK. Sit back and relax.

MAN. Hold your frock up. Up over your face! Shut up!

DEEPAK. Relax and look into my eyes. I am not going to harm you.

MAN. I won't hurt you, I promise.

DEEPAK. Talk to me. Help me to help you.

MAN. Help me and I will love you more than Mummy or Daddy.

DEEPAK. Please!

MAN. I said I am not going to hurt you, stop crying! Shh!

DEEPAK. I love you.

MAN. Think of your school. Be still and put your arms up, come on. Yeees! What did you learn in school today? Hmm? What? Tell me.

DEEPAK *(massaging her arm gently, looking into her eyes)*. You want to be loved but you must trust me.

MAN. Very good. Then sing it. Come on. Sing. Sing!

DEEPAK. You are beautiful.

Deepak embraces her and rocks her as if she is a baby, in a non-sexual way.

MAN. Good. Good. Keep singing . . . Again, don't stop until I stop. See, I love you even though you are so ugly. Keep singing . . . Nobody will tell you how ugly you are. But you are good only for this . . . Only for this. See how much I love you. See . . . Now go away. Quickly.

MALA *(holding him tighter)*. No! Don't go away! Don't leave me!

DEEPAK. I won't. I won't.

Mala breaks away from Deepak and lies on the bed, taking her T-shirt over her head, so that her head is covered and her bra is revealed.

MAN *(now more moralistic than before, the furtiveness gone)*. You like it! You enjoy it. After four years, you have become a whore! At thirteen you are a whore!

MALA. I won't tell anyone. But don't leave me alone!

MAN. Bitch! Whore!

DEEPAK. Mala! No! That's no good! It's no good for you!

The Man leaves in a hurry even as the lights fade on them, but remain on Shanta and the picture.

Deepak pulls her T-shirt back in place and holds her face.

DEEPAK. Mala, you cannot abuse your body like this! I won't let you do it to yourself!

MALA. You don't understand! You cannot understand!

The Man comes back to Shanta's living room. Blackout on Deepak and Mala.

MAN (*to Shanta, as if he has just said something important*). You always go into your own world when I have something important to say to you.

SHANTA. Huh?

MAN. I was saying, that I definitely will do my best to see that this marriage goes through. In spite of her loose ways . . . If only you had controlled her from the beginning. She has always been wayward. You know that.

SHANTA. Yes. I wish I had been more—careful.

Blackout. Deepak's voice on tape plays in the blackout.

DEEPAK'S VOICE. I really wish she would tell me what is on her mind. She doesn't trust me, and I find that very tiring. I am exhausted. I am ready to throw in the towel. If I tell her it's off, she would simply look at me. She may not say a word but her eyes would tell me what she is thinking, 'See. I told you it won't work. You are wasting your time with me. Go away and leave me alone.' But she doesn't want to be left alone. She seeks company. Desperately enough to offer sex in return. Does she really feel anything? I think she wants something else, I don't know what, she doesn't know what . . . it doesn't take our relationship anywhere though . . . I don't even exist for her. I—I am tired . . . (*Sighing.*) I will give it one last shot. I don't know about her uncle . . . I have a strong hunch . . . If what I think is true, then . . . Well, there is only one way to find out . . .

Lights on. Lightning. The doll is fully visible now. We cannot see the doll's face, just its ragged limbs. The dress on the doll is lifted and pinned on to the doll's forehead. The doll remains lit throughout the following scene.

A restaurant. Dinner in progress. Deepak and the Man sit opposite each other. Mala and Shanta sit next to each other. Mala is between her uncle and Shanta. Shanta is between Deepak and Mala.

Music in the background. Vivaldi's Four Seasons. The cutlery and food are all mimed. Shanta and Deepak eat their tandoori roti with their fingers. Mala uses a fork occasionally. The Man uses a knife and fork for eating his chicken breast.

MAN . . . So, when I joined the IT industry, I was thinking of settling in the US. But the real stuff is happening right here.

DEEPAK. True. One can lead a better quality of life right here.

MAN. Yes. Also, we can live our lives the way we want to, without having to be Westernized.

DEEPAK. Yes. Good old Indian values. Where will we be without them?

MAN. In USA.

The Man laughs loudly at his own joke. Deepak laughs too. Shanta smiles. Mala sips her drink.

MAN *(pointing to Mala's empty glass)*. Waiter! Serve more wine here.

SHANTA. No. No. She has had enough.

MAN. You stick to your orange juice. Do you want another one?

SHANTA. No.

MAN. Then keep quiet.

MALA. It's okay, Mummy.

MAN. See. She is a big girl now, as we can all see.

SHANTA. Bhaiya . . .

The Man puts his hand on Mala's shoulder, patting it first, then kneading it.

MAN. What? Have I said anything wrong? The whole world can see she is a big girl. What is there to hide?

Shanta shrinks and looks down at her plate. Mala straightens up.

MALA. Yes. I have been a big girl for fifteen years, Uncle.

MAN. See. She can drink more wine.

The waiter presumably has come with more wine. Mala looks at him with a 'thank you'. The conversation does not stop for this.

DEEPAK. You really seem to be a man of this world, Uncle. You don't mind me calling you Uncle?

MAN. Not at all. If I am Mala's uncle, I can be your uncle, right?

DEEPAK. Right!

SHANTA *(muttering a prayer of thanks to herself)*. If everything goes right ...

DEEPAK. Why shouldn't things go right? Things have been right so far, haven't they? Don't worry.

MAN *(pointing with his fork at Deepak)*. I like you. I like this young man.

DEEPAK. Things have been fine so far. We are all perfect.

Lightning, followed by thunder.

SHANTA. It will rain again tonight.

DEEPAK. You have a great mother and a great uncle.

MAN. Are you being sarcastic?

DEEPAK. As a matter of fact—yes.

MALA. Deepak, what are you getting at?

DEEPAK. Nothing, my dear. Just a few questions that need answers over here.

MAN. Please explain.

DEEPAK. We all know that Mala has been seeing a counsellor. I have too, for her sake.

MAN. If you ask me that is not a good idea. These therapists try to create problems where there are none. It's their job. That is how they earn a living. They will say that 'Oh, because her father left the family . . .'

MALA. What has that . . .?

MAN *(restraining her with a raised hand)*. Then they will blame it all on her father, or her mother. That's what they always do—blame it on the parents and exploit the fact that most people carry some kind of resentment against their parents.

MALA. Just forget he ever brought it up.

DEEPAK. But there is one other person you haven't mentioned.

MALA. Stop it.

SHANTA. Deepak . . .

MAN. No, no. Let us talk about it, now that he has brought it up. If you mean that I have something to do with her depression, then you are wrong. Ask her. I have only given her love and attention, right from the start. I treat her like I would my own daughter.

DEEPAK. She isn't being treated for depression alone . . . It would be interesting to know what happened to her when she was a child. What kind of attention did you give her?

MAN. I am sure your therapist or whoever has set you up for this . . . No, no. It's okay. I understand. It is the fashionable thing to do, blaming whoever was closest to her. But you trust her mother at least. Ask her that question. She will tell you the truth.

MALA. Please! This is embarrassing. Stop it.

MAN *(to Shanta)*. Say something. They are insulting your own brother and you keep quiet.

DEEPAK. What do you have to say about this, Auntie? Remember, the truth is important to me.

MALA. Stop it! Stop it or I will walk out of here.

DEEPAK. Darling, trust me.

MALA. No! I don't want this.

DEEPAK *(to Shanta).* Do you have anything to say about this? Was Mala abused as a child?

Mala gets up to leave.

DEEPAK. I will take your departure and your mother's silence to mean that I have my answer to that question.

Mala stops and turns to Shanta.

MALA. Tell him, Ma.

Shanta looks at Mala and then at Deepak.

SHANTA. You are wrong. There is nothing like that. He is my brother and I know him.

MALA. There. Excuse me, I will be back in a moment.

Mala exits, presumably to the ladies' room.

MAN *(calling the waiter).* The bill please. *(To Deepak.)* I really appreciate your concern for Mala. I mean it. I really do. I think you will make a good husband to her. Believe me, I am not angry with you, but grateful. All she needs is some love and attention and she will be fine. You have my good wishes.

DEEPAK. Thank you. I do apologize for any inconvenience caused to you.

The Man looks at Deepak to see if he is being sarcastic.

DEEPAK. I mean it. I really do.

MAN. Where is that waiter? *(Getting up, mumbling.)* Excuse me, I think I will settle this at the counter.

The Man gets up and exits. Deepak looks at Shanta. Shanta looks away.

DEEPAK *(gently).* I wish you had remained silent.

Blackout. Thunder shower.

The living room. Night. All four enter, a little wet from dashing out of the car and into the building. The sound of the rain can be heard.

MAN. A good end to a perfect evening.

SHANTA. I will get some towels.

Shanta exits in a hurry to get the towels. Mala puts her bag down and remains standing, waiting for the towel.

DEEPAK. Well, that's great for me.

MAN. I am sure your car will be all right in the morning. But relax, we will call a cab for you later. Have another drink.

MALA. You might as well call that cab now. There's nothing in the house to offer you.

Mala goes to the phone and dials the cab service.

MAN. What? No booze? You should have told me, we could have . . .

DEEPAK. It's okay. I think I will be fine.

Shanta enters with the towels and hands them over, while they talk.

MALA *(on the phone)*. This is 1316. Please send a taxi . . . Uday Park. Quickly.

MAN. But do stay for a while. If you have any more questions for us . . .

DEEPAK. No. No. I am sorry. I am embarrassed . . . *(Taking the towel from Shanta.)* Thank you.

MAN *(taking a towel from Shanta and rubbing his head with it)*. Don't be, after all, it shows that you care for Mala.

SHANTA *(to Mala, rubbing her hair with a towel)*. You will catch a cold.

MALA. Give it to me. *(Taking the towel from Shanta.)* Why don't you make us some coffee?

MAN. Splendid idea! Let's drink some coffee since that is all we will get in this house.

Shanta is about to disappear into the kitchen.

MAN. No, wait, Shanta.

Shanta stops.

MAN. I might as well do it now. While Deepak is also here.

SHANTA. What is it?

MAN. Sit down.

Shanta sits down.

MAN. You too, Mala . . . Now, I will be with you in a minute.

The Man exits, while the others remain seated.

Thunder.

SHANTA. It will rain all night!

MALA. What do you think he wants now?

DEEPAK. What do you mean by that?

MALA. What?

DEEPAK. You just said, 'What do you think he wants now?' As opposed to what he wanted then?

MALA. I wasn't thinking of what I was saying.

DEEPAK. That is why it is so telling, what you just said.

MALA *(sharply)*. I don't know what you are talking about! I am not going to that counsellor any more!

DEEPAK. Since there is no problem, why should you go to a counsellor? Right?

The Man enters with an envelope.

MAN. Sorry to keep you all waiting. All I want to say is—I don't know where to begin . . . Shanta is my only sister. I know that life has not been very good to her. Our brothers say that she has brought it upon herself, the loneliness and the—rejection. Her husband left her because—of her . . . But she is my sister and I do have very fond memories of us growing up in our ancestral home. Which unfortunately was sold off by our brothers. So—we only have the pleasant memories to live with now, all of us. I am the oldest in the family and Shanta, the youngest, so I feel it is my responsibility . . . no—that is not the correct way to put it. It's more than a responsibility . . . It is my way of showing my deep and sincere affection to you, my sister.

The Man gives Shanta the envelope. Shanta opens it carefully and removes a legal document. Mala goes to Shanta and looks over her shoulder at the document.

MAN. The title deed. This flat is now yours.

SHANTA *(moved)*. Oh!

MALA. Why? I can pay the rent.

MAN. Yes. But you won't be living here for very long.

MALA. What do you mean?

MAN. I mean you will get married to Deepak and live with him—elsewhere . . . I will be using your room as a spare room for myself when I want to visit Delhi on work. That is if Shanta won't mind. Do you?

SHANTA. Huh?

MALA. You are throwing me out!

MAN. What are you saying? Of course not. You can come and go as you please. It is your mother's flat after all.

Silence, except for the rain and thunder.

MALA. You are throwing me out.

DEEPAK. It's okay, Mala. We will have a home of our own.

MALA *(to Shanta)*. You knew it, didn't you? All along!

MAN. Be reasonable, Mala.

MALA *(to the Man)*. You don't want me—*(Adding.)* here . . .

MAN. You are a grown-up woman now.

MALA. And no good to you . . .

MAN. This is the thanks I get for being so considerate. I didn't expect this response. Not even a 'thank you'?

MALA. Thank you. Oh thank you . . . Thank you, Mother.

The taxi driver honks.

SHANTA. I didn't ask for this, Mala. I did not.

MALA. Yes, you did. He didn't just buy a flat. He bought you!

SHANTA. That's not true! Oh God!

MALA. He bought your silence. So that you can never tell anyone what he did to your daughter!

MAN. You have gone mad.

DEEPAK. Let her speak.

The taxi horn, longer and a little more insistent.

MAN. Your taxi is here. We can talk tomorrow.

DEEPAK *(not moving, staring at the Man).* Go on, Mala.

MALA *(to Shanta).* Where were you when he locked the door to your bedroom while I was napping in there? Where were you during those fifteen minutes when he was destroying my soul? Fifteen minutes every day of my summer holidays, add them up. Fifteen minutes multiplied by thirty or thirty-one or whatever. That's how long or how little it took for you to send me to hell for the rest of my life! Surely you must have known, Ma.

Silence.

MALA. You know, I couldn't say anything to you. You never gave me a chance to. If only you had looked into my eyes and seen the hurt, or asked me, 'Beta, what's wrong?' Then maybe, I would have told you . . . But Ma, I did look to you for help, while you were praying, your eyes avoiding mine and I knew, deep down I must have known, that you will never ask me that question. Because you already knew the answer. *(To Deepak.)* So. You have your answer. But so what? Where do I go from here?

MAN. You really have a wild imagination. That is all I can say.

DEEPAK *(to the Man).* How could you be such a sick bastard?

MAN. You watch your tongue, young man.

DEEPAK *(to Mala)*. It's over, done with. Come with me. Right away.

MALA. You can't really understand me, if you feel it's all over and done with.

Thunder. Followed by a long honk from the taxi.

DEEPAK. What do you mean?

MALA. It can never be over. It won't work between us.

DEEPAK. For God's sake give me a chance and it will. For your own sake.

MALA. For your own sake, forget me.

SHANTA. Go, Mala. Just go with him.

MALA. You know I can't!

DEEPAK. Why not?

MALA. You don't understand! YOU JUST DON'T UNDERSTAND!! I cannot love you.

DEEPAK. Why?

MALA *(looking at the Man)*. Because—because—How can I even begin to explain to you? I see this man everywhere. I can never be free of him. I am not so sure I want to be free of him. Even if I were, I am not sure whether I have the ability to love anyone . . . else.

Silence. Shanta is disturbed. She rises.

SHANTA. What are you saying? What do you mean? You can't love anyone—else? . . . How could you say such a thing? No!

DEEPAK. You don't know what is good for you.

SHANTA *(to Deepak)*. Take her with you. I beg of you. Take her away from this hell. There is no love for her in this house.

MAN. Go, Mala. Go with him. I don't want you. Think of your future.

SHANTA. Mala, you don't know what you are saying. You don't know. Go with him. Learn to love him. Learn ... Forget. Forget. Remember what I told you. Forget!!

MALA. By staying silent doesn't mean I can forget! This is my hell. This hell is where I belong! It is your creation, Ma! You created it for me. With your silence!! You didn't forget anything, you only remained silent!

SHANTA *(defeated)*. Yes. Yes! I only remained silent. I am to blame. That is why God is punishing me today. I remained silent not because I wanted to, but I didn't know how to speak. I—I cannot speak. I cannot say anything. My tongue was cut off ... My tongue was cut off years ago ... *(To Deepak.)* Please save her. I did not save her. I did not know how to save her. How could I save her when I could not save myself? ... *(To Mala.)* You say I did not help you? I could not help you. Same as you could not help me. Did you ever see the pain in my eyes? No. Nobody saw anything. Nobody said anything. Not my brothers, not my parents. Only *(pointing to the Man)* he spoke. Only he said, only he saw and he did.

The man backs away looking at Shanta with a warning.

SHANTA. I was six, Mala. I was six. And he was thirteen ... and it wasn't only summer holidays. For ten years! For ten years!! *(Pointing to the picture of God.)* I looked to Him. I didn't feel anything. I didn't feel pain, I didn't feel pleasure. I lost myself in Him. He helped me. He helped me. By taking away all feeling. No pain, no pleasure, only silence. Silence means Shanti. Shanti. But my tongue is cut off. No. No. It just fell off somewhere. I didn't use it, no. I cannot shout for help, I cannot say words of comfort, I cannot even speak about it. No, I can't. I am dumb. *(To the Man, speaking like a mute person making unintelligible sounds.)* Uh, eh, oo, oo, aa, aa, aaaaaaaaaaa. *(Gesturing with her hands to say she will not tell anyone while making the sounds.)* Aaaaa, ooo eee oooo aaeeeeeeee, aaaaaaaaaaaaaaaaaaaeeeeeeeeee!

Shanta jumps to where the pieces of glass from the portrait are and picks up a sharp piece and jabs it in her mouth. It is all so quick that the rest are shocked.

Mala screams.

DEEPAK. No!

MAN. Shanta!

They try to stop Shanta from doing more harm to herself. Shanta moves away, blood spurting from her mouth. Mala rushes to her with a towel and presses Shanta's mouth with the towel. Shanta looks at Mala with folded hands and falls on her knees. Mala kneels too and holds her. Shanta tries to continue to speak, we only hear muffled sounds as Mala keeps the towel pressed to Shanta's mouth to prevent the bleeding.

MALA. No. Don't speak. Don't say anything. Not now. Not now.

Deepak is on the phone, trying to call the ambulance.

DEEPAK *(since he can't get through)*. Damn! *(Picking up Shanta.)* Quick. Let's take her in the taxi. *(To the Man.)* Help me.

The Man goes to pick up Shanta. Mala stops him.

MALA. Don't you dare touch my mother!

The Man steps back. Deepak and Mala help Shanta up on her feet and take her out of the door to the waiting taxi. The Man looks at them and stays frozen onstage.

Cross-fade to:

The counsellor's office as in the first scene. Mala is seated in exactly the same spot. Mala walks across the stage as the lights cross fade. The Man continues to stand, fixed by a spotlight on him.

MALA *(sighing, thinking about it almost as if it were a pleasant memory)*. I wish he were here now, so I could see his face when I tell him I have nothing to hide. Because I know it wasn't my fault ... Now. I know now.

Pause.

MALA *(saying it with a growing sense of joy).* But what is the point? He is dead. Today. February the 29th, 2004. He is dead. Today. I have made February 29th my Freedom Day. I will celebrate it with my husband. We are going to have a champagne dinner. He is waiting for me this very moment at the restaurant.

The Man remains in his spot. He speaks as a voice in her head and not as the counsellor.

MAN. You look very happy.

MALA. I am.

MAN. And what about your mother?

MALA. What about her?

MAN. Do you still carry any anger against her?

MALA *(thinking about it).* Maybe. But I do see what she has been through. It's been more difficult for her I guess. *(Pause, a little troubled.)* He comes back. He ruined my mother's life too. No matter what I try to do, it all seems to come back to him. I want to forget! I just want to ...

Mala stares at the doll which is now facing her. The Man walks to the doll and picks it up, holding the doll by its skirt so that the skirt covers the dolls face. He rocks the doll while he speaks. Mala looks at the Man.

Silence. Music.

MAN. Touch me here. Quickly, before someone sees you. Touch.

Mala rises, looking at the Man and the doll.

MAN. You said in front of Mummy and Daddy you loved me. Come on! Show it!

Mala hits out at him with her fist. The Man doesn't flinch.

MAN. Don't cry!

MALA *(hitting him hard).* Aaah!

MAN. I said, don't cry!

Mala continues to hit at him each time with more anger as the Man speaks, unaffected by the blows.

MAN. This is our secret! ... Ready for a real birthday present? ... What did you learn in school? Come on, sing it. Sing!

Mala grabs him by the throat and tries to strangle him, heaving with the effort.

MAN. Thirty days has September. April, June, and November. February has twenty-eight. All the rest have thirty-one! Once again. Keep on singing! Stop only when I stop.

MALA *(one last violent shove).* You are dead! You deserve to be dead! Die!

The Man slumps in the chair as if dead. Mala heaves a sigh of relief. Mala picks up the doll, smoothens its dress and comforts it. Spot on Shanta in the temple, beatific. Praying with a sense of peace around her. Cross-fade as Mala speaks. Moving in space. Music continues under Mala's voice. The spot on Shanta in the temple stays. Mala talks while looking at her. Shanta has lit some incense which makes her space appear sanctified somehow, by the smoke. There is a low spot on the Man still in the chair.

MALA. Dear Mother. It just isn't easy to forget. Occasionally I catch his reflection in the glass of a subway, hiding behind a newspaper or pretending to be asleep. But it doesn't matter. I can live with it now. He as a person is not important to me any more.

The spotlight on the Man fades out.

While I accused you of not recognizing my pain, you never felt any anger at me for not recognizing yours. We were both struggling to survive but—I never acknowledged your struggle. Ma, no matter where I am, I always think of you. I want you to know that I am listening. Waiting for you to speak. I promise you I will listen. I am waiting for a sign from you . . . to say that you have forgiven me. Say something. Even a whisper.

The scrim-wall around the prayer room rises. Mala is overjoyed. Shanta continues with her prayer. Mala walks up to her and kneels.

I just want to . . . I want to ask you whether you need my help. Please let me be of help. *(Gently turning her mother's face towards her.)* It's not your fault, Mother. Just as it wasn't my fault. Please, tell me that you've forgiven me for blaming you. Please tell me that.

Shanta turns back to her God and continues with her prayers. Mala slowly rests her head in Shanta's lap.

MALA. I know you will, Mother. I know you have.

Shanta picks up the bell and begins to ring it even as the lights fade out.

Read more in Penguin

COLLECTED PLAYS

Mahesh Dattani

Mahesh Dattani is the first Indian playwright writing in English to be awarded the Sahitya Akademi Award. This volume rings together his first collection of plays that unflinchingly cover a wide range of pertinent issues—sexuality, religious tension, gender inequality—while at the same time focusing on human relationships and personal dilemmas which are the classic concerns of world drama.

Final Solutions, Dance Like a Man and *On a Muggy Night in Mumbai* have been staged to critical and public acclaim all over the country and abroad, and his radio plays, *Seven Steps Around the Fire* and *Do the Needful*, have been aired on BBC Radio. The plays in this collection are prefaced by introductions, which provide fascinating insights into the plays-in-performance in the context of Indian and world theatre.

These eight plays, widely varied in thematic and stylistic content, are a tribute to the dramatic vision and skill of a man who has transformed the face of urban theatre in India.

Drama
Rs 450

Read more in Penguin

COLLECTED PLAYS VOLUME TWO
Screen, Stage and Radio Plays

Mahesh Dattani

Collected Plays Volume Two is essential reading for all theatre enthusiasts. Comprising a rich mix of screen, stage and radio plays by Sahitya Akademi Award-winner Mahesh Dattani, this collection brilliantly displays his talent as a writer and director as well as his wide thematic and stylistic range.

The ten plays in this volume include *Thirty Days in September*, performed extensively in India and abroad to commercial success and critical acclaim, the radio plays aired on BBC Radio and the screenplays of *Mango Soufflé* (winner of the Best Motion Picture award at the Barcelona Film Festival), *Dance Like a Man* (winner of the Best Picture in English awarded by the National Panorama) and *Morning Raga* which premiered at the Cairo Film Festival and won the award for Best Artistic Contribution.

With a general introduction by Jeremy Mortimer of BBC Radio and notes on individual plays by actors like Lillete Dubey and Shabana Azmi, the plays in this collection provide fascinating insights into the human psyche and reveal just how caught up we are in the complications and contradictions of our values and assumptions.

Drama
Rs 450